THE ART OF TRADING THROUGH CANDLESTICK CHARTS

THE ART OF TRADING THROUGH CANDLESTICK CHARTS

SHYAM SUNDAR GOEL

PRABHAT
PRAKASHAN

Published by

PRABHAT PRAKASHAN PVT. LTD.
4/19 Asaf Ali Road,
New Delhi-110002 (INDIA)
e-mail: prabhatbooks@gmail.com

ISBN 978-93-5562-367-6
THE ART OF TRADING THROUGH CANDLESTICK CHARTS
by Shyam Sundar Goel

Edition
2026

Price
₹ 250 (Rupees Two Hundred Only)

Printed at
R-Tech Offset Printers, Delhi

Author's Note

This book represents the culmination of my decades-long journey in the financial markets, with a particular focus on the ancient yet evergreen technique of candlestick charting.

When I first encountered candlestick charts early in my trading career, I was immediately captivated by their visual power and the wealth of information they conveyed at a glance. What began as a curiosity soon became a passion, and ultimately, the cornerstone of my trading strategy.

In this book, I aim to share not just the mechanics of reading candlestick charts, but the art of interpreting them. You'll learn how to spot patterns, understand market psychology, and make informed decisions based on the stories these charts tell.

Whether you're a novice trader looking to build a solid foundation or an experienced investor seeking to refine your skills, this book offers insights that can elevate your trading game. We'll explore everything from basic candlestick formations to complex multi-candlestick patterns, always with an eye toward practical application in real-world markets.

Remember, while candlestick charting is a powerful tool, it's not a crystal ball. It's one piece of a larger trading strategy that should include fundamental analysis, risk management, and a deep understanding of the markets you trade. Use the knowledge in this book as a springboard to develop your own unique approach to trading.

As you embark on this journey, I encourage you to practice patience and persistence. The art of trading is not mastered overnight, but with dedication and continuous learning, you can harness the power of candlestick charts to navigate the markets with greater confidence and precision.

❑

Contents

1

What are Candlesticks?

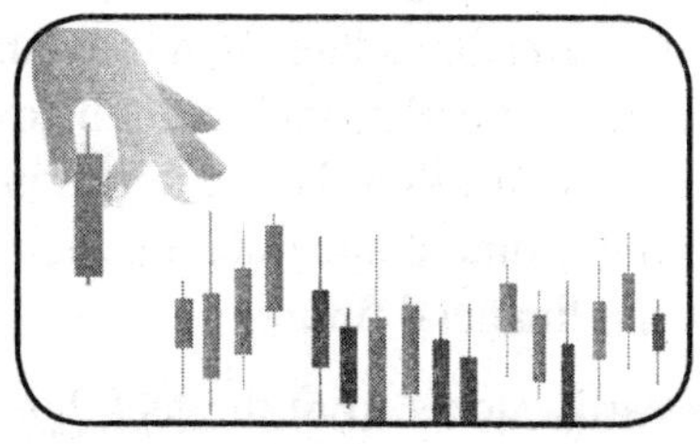

The art of Japanese candlestick trading has been practiced for nearly four centuries. Candlesticks provide a concise way to track price movements and convey extensive data within a single bar. This type of trading has gained widespread popularity among traders because of its simplicity and versatility, enabling the identification of patterns that influence market decisions. Originally developed by Japanese rice traders, these signal formations enabled them to accumulate substantial wealth. Over time, candlestick signals have been refined, tested and applied to various markets. Wherever instruments are traded openly, candlestick signals can be used to generate profits. These signals depict changes in investor psychology, visually representing the traders' sentiments in a particular stock or market. Whether applied to commodities stocks, or futures, candlestick signals are effective across different markets, including Nasdaq, Nikkei, German DAX, and Nifty.

Millions of people across the globe choose to invest their savings in financial markets instead of opting for low-risk, fixed-rate interest-bearing deposits for one simple reason: they want more returns. They dream of financial freedom by building a substantial nest egg for their future, and the prospect of massive returns in the stock market fuels this quest. The reality is that only a tiny subset of investors will make a profit while the bulk pours their money into the market, each investing with the intent that maybe they will get lucky and 'make it big'.

Most traditional investors adhere to a 'buy and hold' strategy, believing in 'averaging down' a stock with the expectation that it will eventually increase in value. They often argue against market timing and spend more time contemplating their daily attire than their investments and financial future.

This mindset partly stems from the fact that real-time access to market data was limited until recently. Investors could only review their investments at the end of the day, and trading costs, such as buying and selling commissions were prohibitively high. However, these factors are no longer relevant. Information technology has revolutionised trading, allowing more people to open online trading accounts with access to real-time data and significantly lower trading costs.

Japanese traders have defined over fifty candlestick signals, but we will focus on the most common ones. These major candlestick signals occur frequently and repeatedly, making them essential for traders and investors to understand.

*****

Candlestick charts, also known as candle charts, are especially useful for spotting early reversal signals. When used correctly, they can help preserve capital while increasing the success rate of trades. Compared to bar charts, candle charts provide a more detailed and accurate market map, opening new avenues of analysis and offering many advantages:

1. Candle charts visually display the supply-demand situation by indicating the ongoing battle between bulls and bears.

2. While bar charts show market trends, candle charts add a dimension by revealing the force behind price movements.
3. Bar charts may take weeks to indicate a reversal, but candle charts often signal imminent reversals within one to three sessions, allowing for more timely trades.
4. Candle charts use the same data as bar charts (open, high, low, close), so all Western technical signals for bar charts can be applied to candle charts. This combination allows traders to get earlier reversal signals while using familiar trading indicators.

For example, if you hold a long stock position and observe the 'Dark Cloud Cover' candle pattern forming, it completes its reversal signal in just two sessions. Recognising this pattern, you might wisely take your gains, especially if other bearish signals confirm it. Those who miss the pattern might continue holding their position, potentially missing out on maximising their profits.

Moreover, candlesticks provide instant insights into market psychology. Early Japanese traders valued understanding market participants' emotions. In today's volatile markets, driven by sudden news and events, awareness of market sentiment is crucial. Unlike bar charts, which do not readily display sentiment, candle charts instantly reveal market sentiment. A candle's extended real body indicates bullish or bearish control, while a small real body shows indecision. These signals are vital for market players and are communicated quickly and efficiently by candlesticks.

*****

The stock market is a game of fear and greed. Supply and demand are just the by-products of these emotions battling for dominance.

Fear creates panic among investors, which increases supply in the marketplace. Greed produces exuberance, driving demand. As humans, we can't escape these emotions while trying to make money in the market.

When your stock declines, fear and anxiety take over. You worry about how much further it could drop, how much you might lose, and what others will think of your losing trade. You're torn between selling now or holding on, fearing a turnaround as soon as you sell.

Conversely, when a stock you want to own rises, greed kicks in. You regret not buying earlier, and worry about missing further gains. You feel compelled to buy because everyone else seems to be profiting.

These emotions are a trader's worst enemy. Experienced traders know they can't master fear and greed. Instead, they design and follow a system to execute their trades, recognising the market's signals. Candlestick signals, with their time-tested market logic, reveal the market's messages.

Stock prices reflect perceived value rather than actual fundamental achievements. Traders should buy into others' fears and sell into others' greed. This contrarian principle is the key to making money in the stock market. Candlestick charts help make this analysis visually apparent.

*****

We will now combine four crucial price points to make one single candlestick to understand how they are drawn. These are the high price, low price, open price and close price of the day. This kind of charting originated in Japan and has successfully been modified over the years which has made it a powerful technical analysis tool in the financial markets.

The Four Key Price Points

1. **High Price of the Day:** The highest price during the trading day for a stock or asset.
2. **Low Price of the Day:** The lowest price during the trading day for a stock or asset.

3. **Opening Price of the Day:** This is the price at which the stock or asset trading begins when the exchange opens the market.

4. **Closing Price of the Day:** This is the price at which the stock or asset trading closes when the exchange closes the market.

The Candlestick Components

A candlestick consists of two main parts: the body and the shadows (or wicks or tails).

The Body

The rectangle body in the centre of the candlestick represents the opening and closing prices for the day. It is critical information on the price movement and the sentiment of the market for that trading session. Depending on this, there can be two types of bodies.

White (Or Green) Body: When the closing price is greater than the opening price, the body is white or green. This implies that the cost of the stock or asset was higher toward the finish of the day than it was at the start, showing bullish sentiment.

Black (Or Red) Body: When the closing price is lower than the opening price, the body colour is black or red. This means that the price of the stock or asset declined during the trading day, demonstrating a bearish market sentiment.

The Shadows

The shadows, or wicks, extend from the body of the candlestick and show the price range beyond the opening and closing prices. There are two shadows: the upper shadow and the lower shadow.

Upper Shadow: The line above the body represents the price range between the highest price of the day and the higher of the opening or closing price.

For a white-bodied candle, the upper shadow extends from the closing price to the high price.

For a black-bodied candle, the upper shadow extends from the opening price to the high price.

Lower Shadow: The line below the body represents the price range between the lowest price of the day and the lower of the opening or closing price.

For a white-bodied candle, the lower shadow extends from the opening price to the low price.

For a black-bodied candle, the lower shadow extends from the closing price to the low price.

Visual Representation

To better understand the candlestick components, let's visualise how they are constructed:

1. White (Green) Candlestick

When a bullish trend is identified, the white candlestick is drawn by plotting the opening price, closing price, high price, and low price for that particular trading period. This candlestick shows that the price of the asset went up during the trading period.

It measures and gives the opening price (the initial trading price of the asset traded at the beginning of the period), closing price (the final trading price of the asset at the end of the period), high price (the highest price reached by the asset during the period), and low price (the lowest price reached by the asset during the period).

Determine and draw the body. Then observe the candlestick body which is the rectangle between the opening and closing prices. When dealing with white candlesticks, where the closing price equals the opening price, it signifies little change in the price—a neutral indicator, reflecting market indecision. Note the opening price on your price axis. Then plot the closing price, ensuring the closing price is higher than the opening price.

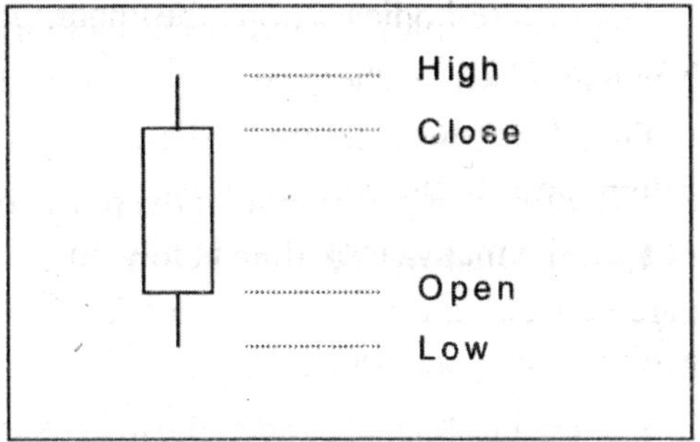

White (Green) Candlestick

Now, mark a rectangle between these two spots. The body will be white or unfilled to show that the asset has increased in price throughout the trading period. Draw the shadows (wicks), Once you have drawn the body, you will then want to append the shadows (or wicks or tails) that represent the traded price area beyond the open and close prices. Start by identifying the high price during that time period. Extend a line from the upper part of the body (close price) up to the high price. This line represents the upper shadow.

Next, identify the low price of the period. Draw a line from the bottom of the body (open price) going down to the low price. This is the lower shadow.

This visual representation indicates that the price of the asset went up during the period, where the upper and lower shadows represent how far the price moved beyond the opening and closing prices.

2. Black (Red) Candlestick

A black (red) candlestick represents a downward trend, with its data encompassing four important price points: the opening price, closing price, high price, and low price of a specific trading period.

This is a kind of candlestick pattern that visually illustrates a situation where the price of the asset has decreased over the trading time frame.

The following are some of the most commonly used elements of a candle many stock traders rely on:

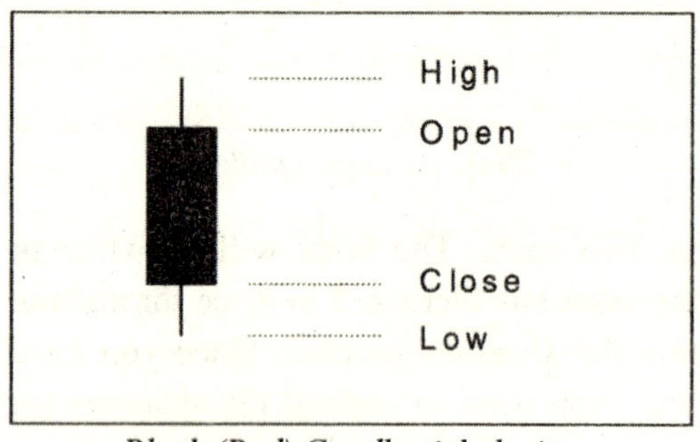

Black (Red) Candlestick depicts

A black or red candlestick is a signal that the closing price is less than the opening price, signalling a downtrend (bearish). Begin by labelling the opening price on your price axis. Next, indicate the closing price which should be below the opening price. Draw a rectangle between two spots: black or red on the body indicates that the price has closed lower than the open. Now to draw the shadows, find the highest price hit during the period. Connect the opening price to the high price to create the higher shadow line. After that, we define the lowest price in this period. Draw a line from the closing price at the bottom of the body down to the low. The line is the lower shadow.

The body of a black or red candlestick is represented by a black or red rectangle, and there is an upper shadow from the opening price (at the top) to the high, and a lower shadow from the closing price (at the bottom) to the low. The asset's price is lower at the end of the time period than at the beginning, and the upper and lower shadows reflect price excursions above and below the opening and closing range. In this case, you get a bit of an insight into what the bearish market sentiment was like at that point in the relevant time frame based on the black or red candlestick.

Advantages of Candlestick Charts

- **Conciseness:** Candlestick charting is very easy to read, meaning price movement and market sentiment are visible.
- **Early signals:** They often provide earlier signals of possible trend changes compared to regular bar charts.
- **Applicability:** Candlestick charts work across all time frames and markets including stocks, futures, forex and commodities.
- **Integration:** Candlestick analysis can be combined with various technical indicators that improve the trading strategies.

There's one more parameter that we'll hear a lot about in the future chapters, so let's discuss that first.

Stochastics

Stochastics, or more specifically the Stochastic Oscillator, is a popular momentum indicator used in technical analysis to determine overbought or oversold conditions in a market. It was developed by George C Lane in the late 1950s.

The Stochastic Oscillator compares a security's closing price to its price range over a specific period of time. It consists of two lines: the %K line and the %D line.

Here's how it's calculated:

1. %K = ((Closing Price - Lowest Low)/(Highest High - Lowest Low)) * 100
   - **Closing Price:** The most recent closing price of the security
   - Lowest Low: The lowest low for the specified period
   - Highest High: The highest high for the specified period
   - %K is typically a 14-period calculation, but this can be adjusted based on the trader's preference.

2. %D = 3-day simple moving average of %K

   - %D is a 3-period moving average of %K. This smoothing helps to reduce the volatility of the indicator.

The Stochastic Oscillator value fluctuates between 0 to 100. Traditionally, readings above 80 suggest the security is overbought, and it could be time for a price correction. Readings below 20 are considered oversold—a security may be undervalued and one would expect prices to come down.

Traders often use signals from the Stochastic Oscillator to guide their own trade decisions. When the %K line crosses above or below the %D line this is known as a crossover—one of the most common signals. For instance, when the %K line crosses above the %D line and both are below 20 (lower than oversold simply by definition), it could be interpreted as a buy signal. Conversely, when the %K is above the %D line and crosses below, it would be considered a sell signal so long as they are both over 80.

The Stochastic Oscillator, like any other technical indicator, is a valuable tool that works best when applied in the context of a broader set of analysis techniques (from candlesticks to oscillators). Traders often use it in addition to other tools that can help them validate trends so that they can spot and determine how to act at potential points of entry and exit of the market.

❑

2

Different Patterns of Candlesticks

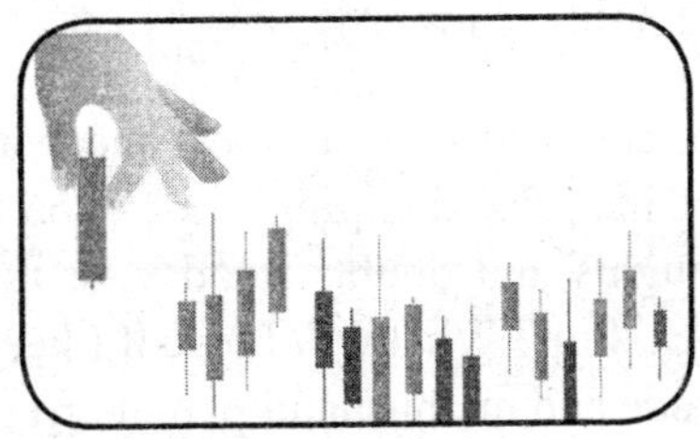

Fear and greed are two of the strongest emotions that drive human behaviour, particularly in financial markets. These emotions manifest distinctly and affect trading decisions to a certain extent. Indeed, understanding how emotions and behaviours related to those emotions interplay with market dynamics, especially when observing candlestick patterns, can offer significant insights among traders and investors.

Fear in the Market

We all know that fear is the most impactful emotion of human beings, which can even create panic, which leads to increased supply in the market. Investors and day traders, driven by fear of prospective losses, often respond by selling off assets. This is often reflected through bearish candlestick patterns. A long red candle, for example, indicates a powerful downward move fuelled by fear and panic in the market. Such patterns suggest that sellers have overwhelmed buyers and are aggressively driving prices lower.

This selling pressure can be driven by a myriad of catalysts such as negative news related to a company, macroeconomic concerns, geopolitical tensions or even rumours. In the field of psychology, these factors influence logical decisions, as negative emotional reactions driven by fear take over. This can lead traders to doubt their decisions and fear potential losses.

For example, say you own a stock and watch as its price declines sharply. This price dumping causes you to drown in fear and anxiety. Thoughts and doubts flood your mind–How much lower can the stock drop? What will I lose if I keep it? Oh, no... If I make a losing trade and my husband/parents/friends know of it... Do I cut my losses and sell now? But what if the stock goes up as soon as I sell it? Wouldn't I feel foolish them?

Those thoughts can create a feeling of panic, which results in you making an impulsive decision to dump the stock. Such panic-driven sales result in the formation of bearish candlestick patterns such as an 'Engulfing Bearish' pattern or a 'Shooting Star' (which indicates a probable change from a bullish to a bearish trend).

The Impact of Greed in the Marketplace

Greed represents the opposite end of the emotional spectrum. Greed leads to euphoria, driving increased demand in the markets. Traders who are motivated by greed typically buy very expensive assets in the hope of making substantial gains. That is generally reflected by the bullish candlestick patterns. For example, a long green candle represents heavy buying pressure, fuelled by greed and the expectation that prices will only go up. These types of formations suggest that buyers outpowering sellers are aggressively driving prices, dominating market sentiment.

There are numerous reasons which drive greed including positive news about a company, favourable economic data presentations, or the fear of missing out (FOMO). When greed comes into play, traders may act impulsively, going long on speculation, hoping to make some gains.

Picture yourself monitoring a stock that has been performing exceptionally well lately for some time now. It is consistently rising now, and you feel a tinge of excitement and greed. You begin to entertain ideas of how awesome the profits will be if we increase our position size, right? But your mind will play a whole list of 'what if' scenarios: Yeah, but how high can this stock go up? The simple question on everyone's mind will probably be: How much more can I earn if I invest more? What happens if this stock becomes the next best thing and I lose my chance to invest?

This thinking leads to a hurried increase in purchasing more shares. This buying due to greed leads to the formation of various bullish candlestick patterns like the Engulfing Bullish pattern or the Hammer which signify a possibility of a change in trend from bearish to bullish phase.

The Interplay of Fear and Greed

Fear and greed often work together in many sophisticated ways, impacting market behaviour and trading moves. The ever-changing balance of these emotions establishes a competitive space, in which prices wildly oscillate from one sentiment to another.

For example, if the cryptocurrency had been increasing in value for an extended period as a result of greed, then traders may eventually start fearing an imminent downturn where their investments could deflate due to market conditions. Bearish candlestick patterns can be indicative of such a sentiment shift and mark the turning of a trend. In contrast, after a long stressed sell-off driven by fear and panic, greed begins to reemerge among investors who see opportunities to purchase undervalued assets. This change in mood can lead to the formation of bullish candlestick patterns that indicate a probable upswing in the market.

Unfortunately, as humans, we cannot avoid these two emotions when it comes to making money in the marketplace. The question is how we recognise, manage and integrate these emotions into our decision-making process, rather than allowing them to dictate our actions impulsively.

Psychological Impacts on Trading Decisions

The psychological impact of fear and greed on trading decisions cannot be overstated. These emotions can cloud judgement, leading to irrational behaviour and suboptimal outcomes. To better understand how fear and greed affect trading, let's delve into the psychological mechanisms at play.

1. **Fear and Loss Aversion**: Loss aversion is a well-documented psychological phenomenon where individuals prefer avoiding losses over acquiring equivalent gains. When faced with the possibility of a loss, fear intensifies, leading to panic selling. This behaviour is evident in candlestick patterns that show sharp declines, reflecting the collective anxiety of traders trying to avoid further losses.

2. **Greed and Overconfidence**: Greed often leads to overconfidence, where traders believe they can predict market movements and make profitable trades consistently. This overconfidence can result in excessive risk-taking and speculative buying, which is reflected in bullish candlestick patterns. However, overconfidence can also lead to complacency, making traders vulnerable to sudden market reversals.

3. **Emotional Contagion**: Emotions are contagious, and in financial markets, fear and greed can spread rapidly among

traders. News, social media, and market rumours can amplify these emotions, leading to collective behaviour that drives market trends. This phenomenon is visible in candlestick patterns that show abrupt changes in market sentiment.

While it is impossible to eliminate fear and greed entirely, traders can take steps to mitigate their impact by developing a structured trading plan, setting realistic goals, practicing mindfulness, utilising technical analysis, maintaining a trading journal, and implementing risk management techniques. By doing so, traders can make more informed decisions, navigate market fluctuations with greater confidence, and ultimately improve their chances of success in the marketplace.

*****

Candlestick signals, by their very nature, provide insights into market sentiment. Developed and refined over a period of four centuries, these signals continue to endure because they are grounded in strong market principles.

Candlestick signals serve as reflections of the collective sentiment and perception of traders and investors towards a stock. Often, the stock prices are influenced more by the 'perceived' fundamentals than the actual fundamentals. Even if a company has strong fundamentals and a track record of success, if market participants are uncertain that the company will be able to grow over time, the stock may not see significant gains.

Would you invest more in an established company with steady growth potential or an emerging stock perceived to have explosive growth prospects? Most would choose the latter. That is what makes the stock market so exciting. This fear of loss and greed for gain are responsible for every price imbalance that happens in the stock market; this dynamic creates demand-supply imbalances that cause stock prices to rise and fall.

If there is one take-home lesson from this book, let it be the lesson to buy when others are fearful and sell when they are greedy as both of these extremes offer strong evidence that a turn in market direction is imminent.

*****

As we have already discussed how white and black candlesticks with shadows are formed, you might wonder what it means when a candlestick has no shadows at all. These special types of candlesticks are known as White Marubozu and Black Marubozu.

White Marubozu

This pattern occurs when the day's low price matches the opening price, and the day's high price matches the closing price. Typically, this configuration signals a strong bullish trend, indicating that the bulls dominated the market throughout the day.

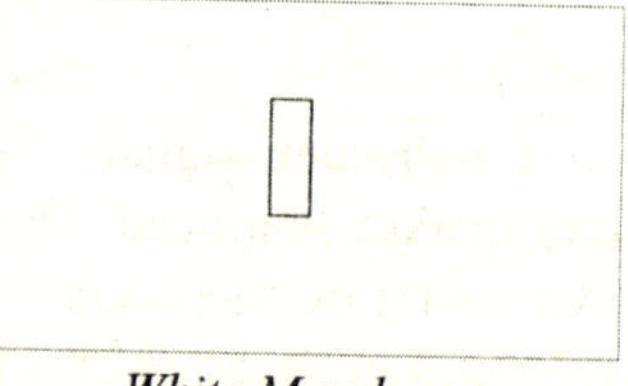

White Marubozu

Black Marubozu

A Black Marubozu is a bearish candlestick pattern that also has no shadows, meaning it opens at the highest price of the period and closes at the lowest price of the period. This reflects strong selling pressure throughout the trading session.

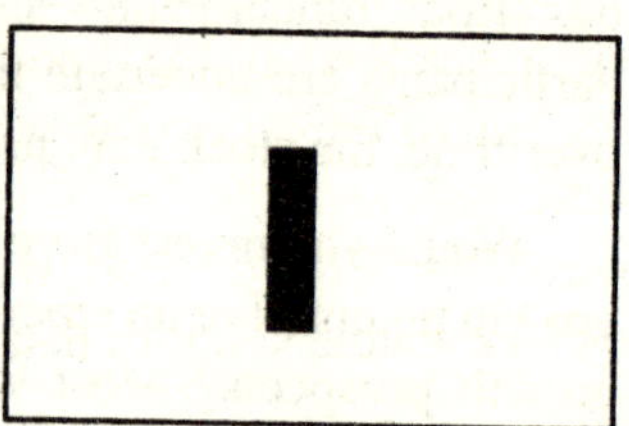

Black Marubozu

Key Takeaways

White Marubozu: It shows a very strong bullish trend with no hesitation to enter and buy.

Black Marubozu: Strong bearish trend due to no respite from sellers.

These two patterns are strong market sentiment signals and both can used to predict future price trends. They are distinct indications of what the overall feeling is; whether it is all bullish (White Marubozu) or all bearish (Black Marubozu). Traders can capitalise on this phenomenon, and use these patterns to either confirm the strength of the market trends or to make educated guesses about when it might end.

Opening and Closing Morubozu

Opening Marubozu

The Opening Marubozu is simply a candlestick pattern opening at either the high or low of the period and featuring a shadow on one end.

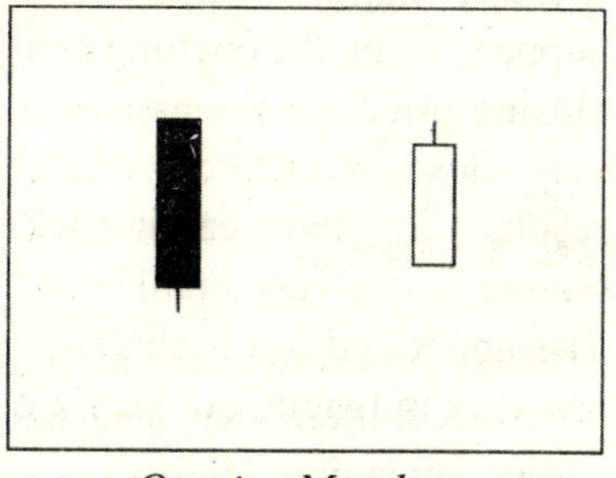

Opening Marubozu

As you can see, these candles lack a shadow at the opening price end of the body. The white candle indicates that bulls took control right from the start, while the black candle signifies that the bears dominated from the open.

Closing Marubozu

A Closing Marubozu is a candlestick pattern when the closing price is equal to the high or low of the day.

As can be seen, the Closing Marubozu does not have a tail attached to the closing price end of the body.

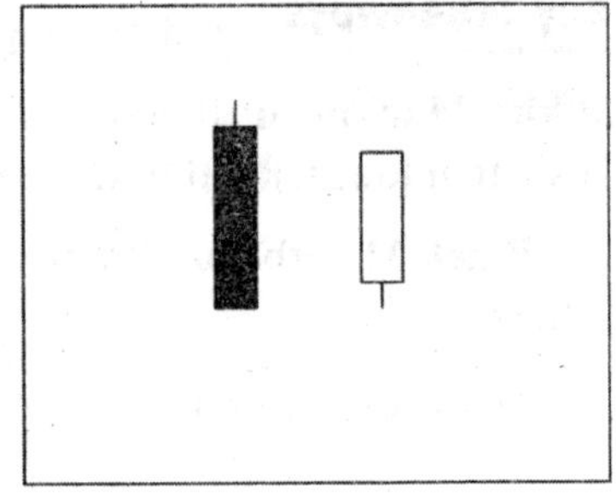

Closing Marubozu

The white candle implies that the bulls took control during the day and ended the day strong. Conversely, the black candle suggests that the bears took over during the day and forced the price to close at the lowest level of the day.

Now let's move to a very important indicator which is called a Doji.

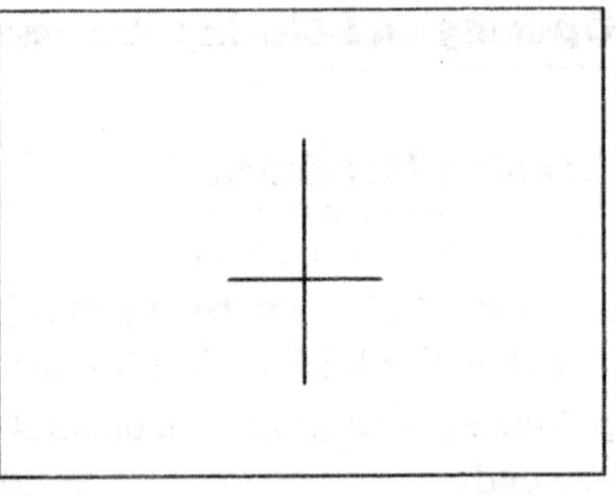

Doji signal

Doji is an important candlestick in candlestick charting usually indicating indecision or a probable reversal in the trend. This happens when the opening and closing prices of the asset are very close or identical which results in the candlestick having no or a very small body. The upper and lower shadows can vary in length, but they are typically longer than the body.

Doji consists of various types such as:

Standard Doji: The opening price and closing price are almost the same. This quite literally signals a (buy/sell) tug of war where the bulls and bears are battling each other, and hence it calls for indecision in the market.

Long-Legged Doji: Both the upper and lower shadows are longer than the body, signalling even more indecision. This suggests that the trading range was wide, but it closed near the opening price.

Dragonfly Doji: This candlestick has a long wick at the bottom but it doesn't have one on top, which shows that buyers were able to control the price for the day, but they couldn't raise it higher than they started with. It is considered to be a potential reversal to the upside.

Gravestone Doji: This is characterised by a very long upper shadow and no lower shadow, which means buyers were able to push the price higher after the opening, but by the close of the session, sellers managed to push the price back to the opening level. This nearly always indicates an incipient downtrend.

A Doji after a strong uptrend or downtrend may signal a potential reversal, especially if it is accompanied by other technical indicators or candlestick patterns. Traders often look for confirmation from subsequent price action before making trading decisions based on Doji patterns.

Before delving into the intricacies of candlestick charts, let's first find out why candlestick charts are preferred.

One of the most frequently used charts to conduct technical analysis and visualise price fluctuations across financial markets are line charts, as well as candlestick charts. Although both have their benefits, candlestick charts tend to be preferred due to the extra insight they offer into pricing behaviour. They are compared here.

Representation of Price Data

Line Chart: A line chart connects each closing price of each period with a line. It is a basic formulation of volume-adjusted price movement for a given time period which makes visible the general price trend over time.

Candlestick Chart: Candlestick charts show four price points for each time period; open, high, low and close. The body tells us the range between the open and close, while the shadows (also known as wicks) tell us both high and low prices.

Information Density

Line Chart: They give a very limited amount of information, showing you only the closing prices. They lack detailed information such as trading range and price volatility data in the context of each period.

Candlestick Chart: Candlestick charts are more detailed and provide the open, close, high and low of a day's trading. Traders can use the additional data to analyse market sentiment and price movements.

Visual Clarity

Line Charts: Line charts are minimal and straightforward visual representations that are useful for detecting overall trends over extended periods.

Candlestick Charts: Candlestick charts display multiple price points for each time period along with a very visually complex way to see the information. Nonetheless, they do illuminate more granular changes in prices—a useful detail for traders making decisions over the short term.

Overall Preference

Candlestick charts are generally favoured by traders and analysts because can provide a more detailed view of price action compared to line charts. They are particularly useful for day traders and those employing technical analysis strategies and work well with patterns they can identify on the charts.

To sum up, line charts are simple and easy to understand, but many traders prefer candlestick charts for a comprehensive picture of price action that they can use to conduct technical analysis.

❑

3

Different Signals

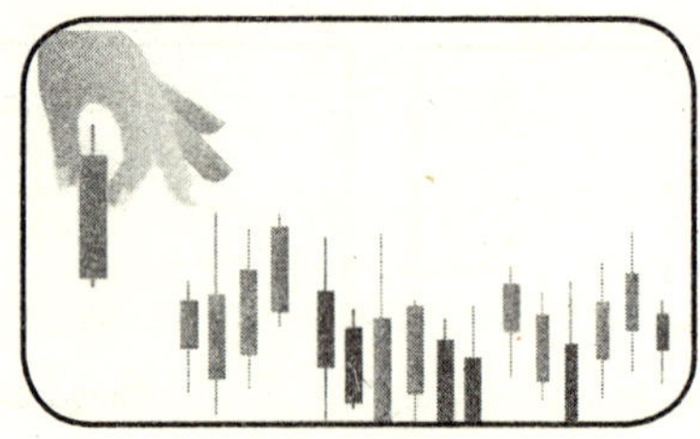

Now moving forward, let's delve into different kinds of signals. The first that we will study is the Doji signal.

Doji is a significant candlestick pattern in technical analysis representing a state of market indecision. As per the Japanese candlestick charting principles, the appearance of a Doji should be watched carefully as it suggests an indecision/ reversal or potential reversal in market sentiment.

When the asset opens and closes at almost the same price, a Doji is formed with little or no body and upper and lower shadows. This gets you the following pattern—an equilibrium between buyers and sellers where neither has really gained control. Therefore, Doji patterns are most found at key points in the market, indicating indecision among market participants and potential reversals or pauses in the prevailing trend.

When in tandem with other technical indicators, the appearance of the Doji on a price chart is open to interpretation by traders and analysts. For instance, a Doji after a strong uptrend or downtrend might signal a near-term reversal if confirmed by other signals like volume analysis or trendline breaks.

The Doji is said to be the most powerful signal in Japanese candlestick charting and it should not be overlooked or ignored.

There are some variations that we need to discuss further in the Doji signal.

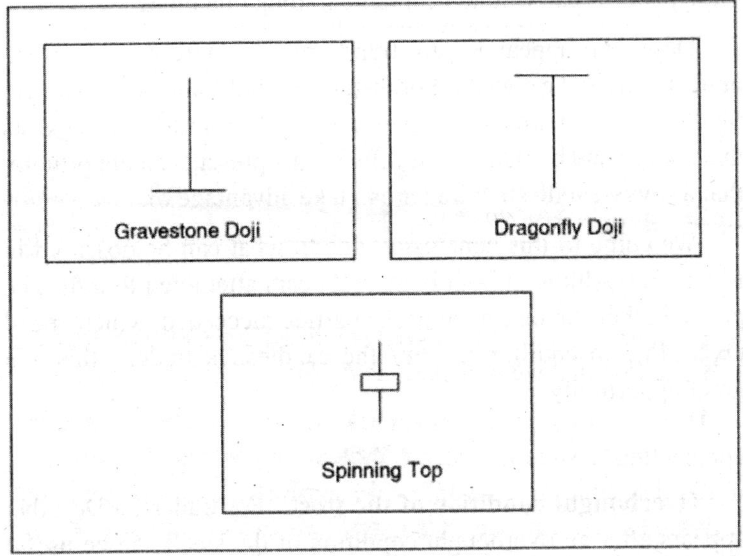

Doji variations

A Gravestone Doji is characterised by a long upper shadow and no lower shadow. The candlestick resembles a gravestone, hence the name. The analogy of 'soldiers advancing during the day and retreating to their original positions at night' illustrates the market dynamics illustrated by the Doji. This particular Doji works very well at the tops of trends, signalling potential reversals because of an inability to push the price higher again.

A Doji without an upper wick is known as a Dragonfly Doji as it resembles a dragonfly. This is a bullish pattern at the bottom of a trend, with sellers trying to push the price lower during the trading session, but buyers eventually bring it back up to near the opening level by the close.

A Doji with a small body is called a Spinning Top. These names are just for informational benefit. They have no importance in candlestick trading. The interpretation of the candlestick patterns is what matters most. The skillful interpretation and application of these patterns can lead to profitable trading outcomes.

Dojis can appear in any trend and are more reliable when understanding the context. For instance, if bulls and bears battle to tip the scales towards themselves but end at a standstill, it suggests that supply and demand are levelled. This presents an opportunity that a savvy candlestick trader can take advantage of.

We come to this conclusion due to what can be observed in Figure 3.2. Although both bulls and bears attempted to influence prices in their favour, none of the parties succeeded, which ended up leading to equilibrium. For the candlestick traders, this is a great opportunity.

*****

Overbought condition of the stock: For traders, a Doji that appears after an overbought condition of the stock can be useful information. According to Japanese candlestick analysis, this means that a local reversal in the trend is brewing. A rising stock with white candles reflects positive movement. Then, suddenly, a Doji forms. This analogy of the bears who 'catch the falling knife so hard that their hands bleed a little' illustrates how a Doji reflects a shift in sentiment. Despite attempts by bulls to push the price higher, they fail to sustain momentum. If the price opens lower the next day, it means that the bulls have capitulated and a reversal is at hand.

Oversold condition of the stock: In a different situation, a Doji in an oversold stock can also suggest that the downtrend is coming to an end and a reversal is looming. In this case, bears are in control as you can see from the black candles. In some cases, especially when the bulls hold a support level and manage to create a Doji, it simply means that the bears start doubting their positions.

Stock trading sideways in a range: If the stock is trading sideways within a range, Doji candles can signal a temporary pause in the market and can show an early step towards a new trend. A long Doji candle after a prolonged sideways movement period usually indicates that the price has moved to the right place between demand and supply. A gap up or gap down the next day by the market can confirm this breakout and signal the start of a new trend. This is mainly because after a Doji, traders have decided which side of the coin is stronger (bulls or bears) with much greater certainty and it validates the potential beginning of a new trend.

*****

Japanese trading wisdom, however, says that a Doji at the top of a trend gives a very strong signal to SELL right away. This pattern also signals that a trend reversal almost becomes a possibility because bulls are losing control while bears may be gaining strength. Traders interpret this as a warning sign that the uptrend may be nearing its trend and that a downtrend or at least a correction could follow.

However, when a Doji occurs at the bottom of a bear market, the scenario is different and requires careful analysis. For the time being, the bears have been dominant and pushed the prices lower. Now at this point if a Doji is formed, it signifies indecision in the market, It could mean that the bears are losing momentum. To confirm a potential trend reversal from bearish to bullish, the bulls need to break above with a strong bullish candlestick pattern or any other confirmation signals. These confirmations are crucial as they validate that the bulls are gaining control and are likely to push prices higher.

Hammer and Hanging Man Signals

Both the Hammer and Hanging Man are important one-day reversal signals with candlestick chartings. The aforementioned patterns used in technical analysis can provide signs of a possible trend reversal. But always remember, if you need these signals in order to enter into trades, they must be confirmed by using additional technical analysis tools and indicators.

The Hammer candlestick is a bullish reversal pattern and is formed in a downward trend. It has a small body with little or no upper shadow and a longer lower shadow. This suggests that sellers pushed the prices lower during the session, but buyers regained control, pushing prices back up. This indicates a probable bullish reversal. Traders have to wait for confirmation on the following trading session, i.e., the open should be higher than the Hammer candle's close, and a bullish candlestick should follow the Hammer.

You can see this by comparing the two patterns: a Hammer (or even an Inverted Hammer, it does not matter; both have the same meaning) has a small body and a small lower shadow but no upper shadow. Meanwhile, the Hanging Man pattern shows a small body too but in this case with an upper shadow. This pattern gives the impression that buyers drove the price up in the session but sellers pushed it back down hence a potentially bearish reversal.

Hammer Signal Criteria

For the Hammer signal to be considered valid, several conditions must be met:

1. The price must have been in a clear downtrend before the Hammer signal occurred, which should be visually identifiable on the chart.
2. The lower shadow of the Hammer should be at least twice the size of the body.

3. The day after the Hammer forms, there should be continued buying pressure.
4. There should be no upper shadow or only a very small one. The colour of the body (white or black) is not as important, but a white body is more positive than a black body.

The reason why a Hammer pattern signals a reversal is that it represents the moment when the selling pressure has been exhausted. The buyers now start to enter and drive up the price of the financial instrument. Think of a stock that has been in a downtrend, causing investors to experience heartache and panic-sell, sending the price massively low intraday. But well into the day, smart money comes back in, with the belief that the stock is undervalued and the price starts rising again, pushing it up at least close to the open price causing a Hammer. The term 'hammering out a bottom' describes this scenario, where the Hammer indicates that the stock has reached a temporary bottom. Traders should wait for confirmation that the stock traded higher on the following day, confirming the reversal and bulls wrested back control.

Additionally, certain conditions can make the Hammer signal more compelling as a buy signal:

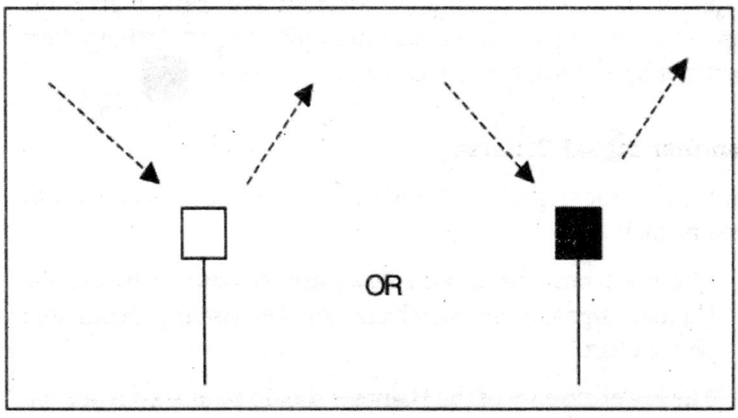

Hammer Signal

1. A gap down from the previous day's close on the day of the Hammer.
2. A spike in volume on the day of the Hammer.
3. The Stochastic Oscillator, a technical momentum indicator, shows that the stock is in an oversold condition.
4. The longer the lower shadow of the Hammer, the stronger the signal.

The Hammer and Hanging Man signals are similar in formation but differ in their positions within a trend. The Hammer occurs after a downtrend, signalling a potential reversal to the upside, while the Hanging Man appears after an uptrend, indicating a possible reversal to the downside.

Hanging Man Signal Criteria

For the Hanging Man signal to be valid, several conditions must be met:

1. The stock must have been in a clear uptrend before the signal occurs, which should be visually verifiable on the chart.

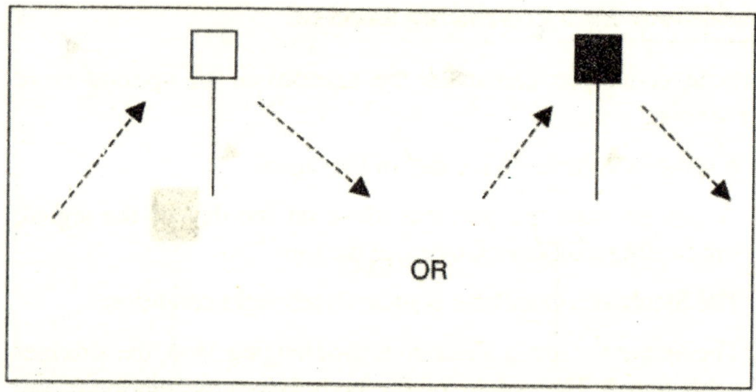

Hanging Man Signal

2. The lower shadow of the Hanging Man should be at least twice the size of the body.
3. The day after the Hanging Man signal should witness continued selling pressure and a lower close.
4. There should be no upper shadow or only a very small one.

Why the Reversal Works

As the value of your portfolio increases, investors and traders become more optimistic, especially during an uptrend. But when the entities holding a significant portion, say 40% of the outstanding shares, decide to sell some of their holdings, selling pressure is introduced in the market. Beginner investors, seeing a temporary dip in the stock, may interpret it as a buying opportunity. Their buying actions help to stabilise the price and move it back towards the earlier highs. As the stock fails to regain its highs, the bulls become nervous and as their confidence fades, they grow fearful of losing gains instead of being motivated by future gains. The next day the stock closes lower, which only confirms their fears. This leads to further selling pressure as the bears finally take control.

Conditions for a Convincing Reversal

Several conditions can make the reversal of an uptrend more convincing:

1. A spike in volume on the day of the signal.
2. A gap up from the previous close on the day of the signal, indicating exuberant buying at the top.
3. The Stochastic Oscillator is in an overbought condition.
4. The longer the lower shadow of the Hanging Man, the stronger the signal. The colour of the body is not as important, but

a black body would provide a stronger confirmation of the reversal.

Inverted Hammer and Shooting Star Signals

The Inverted Hammer and the Shooting Star signals are both one-day reversal signals that are essentially the opposite of the Hammer and the Hanging Man signals, respectively.

Inverted Hammer

The Inverted Hammer is found near the bottom of a downtrend and signals a potential reversal to the upside.

Criteria for Inverted Hammer

1. The stock must have been in a clear downtrend before the signal occurs.
2. The upper shadow of the Inverted Hammer must be at least twice the size of the body.
3. The day following the Inverted Hammer should witness continued buying pressure.

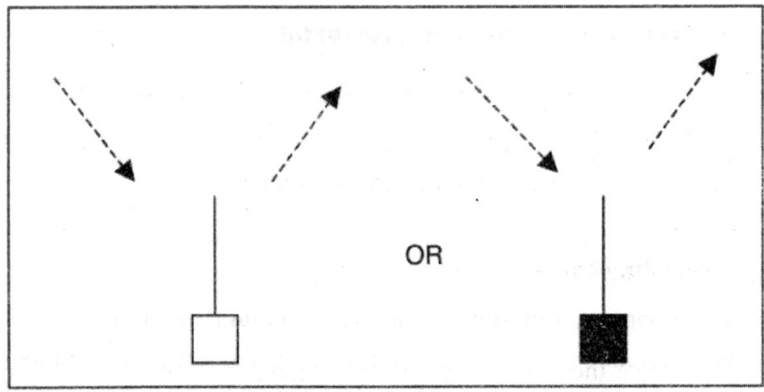

Inverted Hammer signal

4. There should either be no lower shadow or only a very small one. The colour of the body is not as important, but a white body would be more positive than a black body.

Why the Reversal Works: When portfolios are in the red, panic takes over, incentivising investors to sell their positions. This selling pressure prompts smart money investors to buy the dip. When the stock opens flat or even slightly down despite previous selling pressure, the bulls step in and push the prices higher throughout the day. Despite the bears pushing the price lower again by the close, clearly there are bulls in town. If the bulls can lift the price above the previous day's close by the end of the session, it indicates a potential change in trend. The peak must be approximately twice (2x) the size of the body to show bull power at the Inverted Hammer. Ideally, the body of the candlestick must be white, indicating that the bulls managed to close above the open.

Conditions for a Compelling Buy Signal

1. A gap down from the previous day's close on the day the Inverted Hammer forms.
2. A spike in volume on the day of the Inverted Hammer.
3. The Stochastic Oscillator is in an oversold condition.
4. The longer the upper shadow of the Inverted Hammer, the stronger the dominance shown by the bulls.

Shooting Star

The Shooting Star signal is a bearish reversal pattern that forms after an uptrend. The signal looks like a shooting star with its tail pointing to the sky, hence the name.

Criteria for Shooting Star

1. The stock must have been in a clear uptrend before the signal occurs. This can be visually confirmed on the chart.
2. The upper shadow of the Shooting Star must be at least twice the length of the body.
3. The day following the Shooting Star should witness continued selling pressure and a lower close.
4. There should be little to no lower shadow.

Why the Reversal Works: Inexperienced investors buy stocks at the top because they believe that the stock will keep rising. This euphoria creates a powerful up move, giving birth to a white long-body candlestick at the end of the day. When this happens, smart money who may have been shorting the stock, start selling their positions. This creates a candlestick with a long upper shadow, known as the Shooting Star. If the stock closes lower the next day, it confirms that an uptrend has reversed. The bulls were back in control at the open, but by the end of the day, the bears had wrestled away control as evidenced by a long upper shadow.

Conditions for a Convincing Reversal

1. A spike in volume on the day of the Shooting Star signal.
2. A gap up from the previous close on the day of the signal, indicating exuberant buying at the top.
3. The Stochastic Oscillator is in an overbought condition.
4. The longer the upper shadow, the stronger the indication of bearish reversal.
5. While the colour of the Shooting Star's body does not matter, a black body would be a stronger confirmation of the reversal.

Critical to a trader's success is the mastery over candlestick patterns to aid in weighing out your decision! Of these patterns, the Doji, Shooting Star, Hammer and Inverted Hammer are critical reversal signals from which you can garner essential information on market sentiment and potential price directions. Getting a grip of these patterns and understanding how they respond can make or break your trading strategy.

The Importance of Candlestick Patterns

Candlestick patterns provide a visual representation of price movements over short time frames. The opening, closing, high and low prices are grouped as individual candles each portraying a view of the market trends in short time frames. These patterns are so powerful because they encapsulate the sentiment of market participants. Identify and translate these patterns to leave behind the curve balls of predictable reversals, and dive into your trades with greater confidence.

The Doji

One of the most significant signals in a candlestick chart analysis is the Doji. This happens when the opening and closing prices are almost equal, making the body very small or even non-existent. The Doji shows indifference as the bulls and bears have fought to a draw. The Japanese always say that wherever you see a Doji, be alert as it signals a significant move in the market.

The Doji can be found in all market conditions, but its meaning depends on its placement in the market trend. When a Doji forms during an uptrend, it shows that the bullish momentum might be weakening. On the other hand, when a Doji appears at the peak of an uptrend, it may suggest a bearish reversal ahead and that the bulls have run out of steam. Conversely, when a Doji appears at the bottom of a downtrend, it might be symbolic of impending bullish sentiment. In either case, traders should wait for confirmation. The Doji at the top of the market with a lower opening is considered a valid reversal signal to the bearish side, while the Doji at the bottom of a market with a higher opening reflects a valid bullish reversal.

The Shooting Star

The Shooting Star is a bearish reversal signal after an uptrend. This price pattern has a small body and a long upper shadow, resembling a star falling from the sky. Ideally, the upper shadow should be about two times or more the size of the body and very little to no lower shadow.

A Shooting Star formation reveals that despite healthy buying pushing prices higher, sellers stepped in to take profits, causing prices to retreat from their highs. This reversal in price momentum from upward to downward can signify the uptrend nearing its end. Traders look for follow-up selling the following day where a lower close only adds to the downside confirmation.

The Hammer

A trend reversal signal, the Hammer forms after a downtrend. It has a small body and a long lower shadow to indicate that sellers pushed prices lower during the day but buyers entered the market aggressively and pushed the price back up towards the opening price or higher. The lower shadow must be twice as long as the body and there should be no upper shadow, or a very small one.

If a Hammer is present, this would suggest that we may be near the bottom of a downward trend and buyers are beginning to take over. To confirm the bullish reversal signal signalled by the Hammer, the closing price should be higher than the high of the Hammer. This validates the bullish bias.

The Inverted Hammer

The Inverted Hammer is similar to the Hammer but a downtrend must precede it and it has a long upper shadow instead of a lower. This pattern implies that buyers attempted to push the price higher during the trading session, but sellers pushed the price back down near the opening price. The upper shadow must be a minimum of twice the length of the body and there should be little to no lower shadow.

The Inverted Hammer indicates that the sellers are losing their grip on the trend and buyers may be poised to take control. This is confirmed when the next day continues with bullish pressure and ends with a higher close (not shown). It is a sign that the bulls are getting stronger and the downtrend may reverse.

How These Reversal Patterns Work

This is how reversal patterns such as Doji, Shooting Star, Hammer and Inverted Hammer function as tools to detect shifts in market sentiment. These patterns show the ongoing battle between the buyers and sellers and when one side is starting to take control. Traders who can spot these signals early can potentially anticipate trend reversals and adjust their trading positions accordingly.

When the Doji appears, it is time for indecision and possible reversal. The Shooting Star shows potential exhaustion among buyers and a possible trend reversal from bullish to bearish. Both the Hammer and Inverted Hammer indicate that buyers have started to battle for control after a downtrend, indicating a potentially bullish reversal.

Reacting to Candlestick Signals

To trade these candlestick signals with high probability, traders will need confirmation before they enter a trade. If a Doji is at the top, then confirmation is provided by a lower opening and continued selling. A Doji at the bottom requires a higher opening with a strong plus-up day for confirmation. A lower close the next day confirms the Shooting Star's bearish reversal and higher closes confirm the Hammer and Inverted Hammer's bullish reversals.

Traders should not only look for whether the level has been confirmed but also evaluate volume, gaps, and stochastics among other technical metrics. A high volume day accompanied by the signal reinforces the reversal and gaps can impart information about how traders are positioned. Trade signals can be further confirmed by identifying overbought-to-oversold conditions on stochastics.

❑

4

The Engulfing Signals

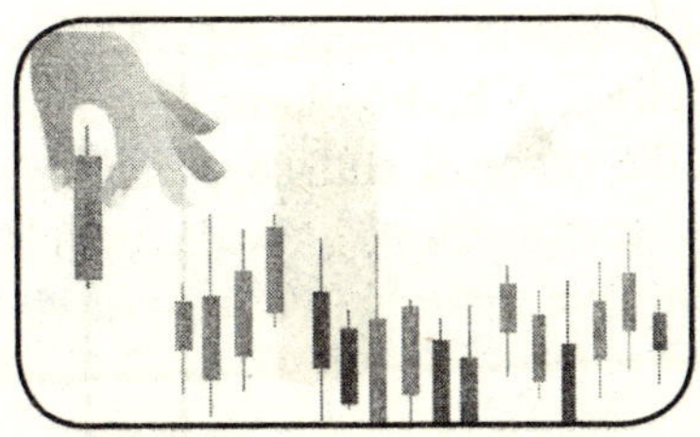

Engulfing candlestick patterns are strong two-day reversal setups that allow traders to pick up on potential market turns. These signals are of two types: Bullish Engulfing and Bearish Engulfing. Let's delve into the Bullish Engulfing pattern—what it looks like, how it works, and how you can use this signal to make better trades.

The Bullish Engulfing Pattern

The Bullish Engulfing pattern is a powerful reversal signal that occurs when the market has been in a downtrend. Basically, there are just two candles—a smaller bearish candlestick followed by a larger bullish candlestick. This candlestick pattern features a bullish candle that has fully engulfed the entire bearish candle. This engulfing action is a reversal in market sentiment from bearish to bullish, signalling that buyers have overwhelmed sellers.

Criteria for Validity

To validate the Bullish Engulfing signal, certain conditions must be met:

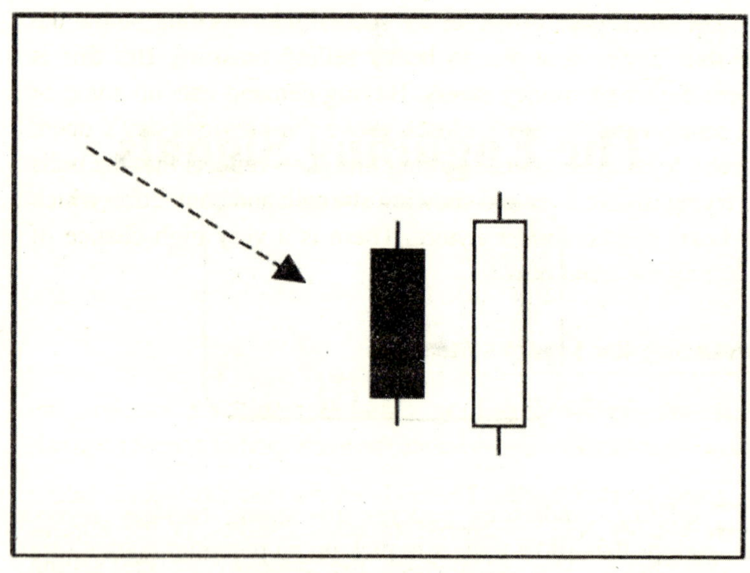

Bullish Engulfing signals

1. **Downtrend Preceding the Signal**: The stock should have been in a clear downtrend before the appearance of the Bullish Engulfing pattern. This downtrend can be visually confirmed on the chart.

2. **Engulfing White Candle**: On the second day of the signal, a white (bullish) candle must completely engulf the body of the previous day's black (bearish) candle. Even if the first day is a Doji (as described in Chapter 3), it still qualifies as a Bullish Engulfing signal.

Why the Reversal Works: Imagine a stock that has been declining steadily over a prolonged period, causing anxiety among investors as they watch their portfolios diminish day by day. Those investors hope for a turnaround, but after ongoing losses, finally give up and sell. This mass exit usually occurs at the low that forms the long black candle of day one.

The stock gaps down on the second day, opening below the previous day's close due to heavy selling pressure. But this is where the smart money enters. Buying demand eats up some of the supply, and the stock closes above the previous day's open, thereby forming a white engulfing line. This reflects that the bulls are trying to take over and showing strength and conviction which the bears can no longer ignore. There is a very high chance of reversing the trend now.

Enhancing the Signal's Strength

While the Bullish Engulfing signal is robust on its own, the following conditions can enhance the likelihood of a trend reversal:

1. **Long Dark Candle**: The body of the first day's dark candle is notably long compared to other candles in the current downtrend. This emphasises the intensity of the selling pressure before the reversal.

2. **Volume Spike**: There is a noticeable spike in volume on either of the two signal days (dark candle day or white engulfing candle day), indicating strong participation by traders and adding credibility to the reversal.

3. **Gap Down**: The first dark candle should gap down from the previous trend, highlighting the desperation of the remaining panic sellers to exit the stock.

4. **Oversold Stochastics**: Stochastics should be in an oversold condition, suggesting that the stock is due for a rebound as selling pressure has likely been exhausted.

5. **Multiple Candles Engulfed**: The second day's white candle engulfs more than one black candle from the previous trend, reinforcing the bullish reversal.

This is a clear reversal signal that could mark a period of profit for traders: the Bullish Engulfing pattern. Traders can make judgements by evaluating the changing market sentiment and knowing what contributes to the strength of that signal. Bullish Engulfing patterns not only indicate a change in direction but also reflect the transformation of market sentiment from fear to confidence which can result in some pretty sharp moves.

Formation and Criteria of the Bullish Engulfing Pattern

To identify a valid Bullish Engulfing pattern, certain criteria must be met:

1. **Downtrend Preceding the Pattern**: The market should be in a clear downtrend before the appearance of the Bullish Engulfing pattern. This downtrend sets the stage for a potential reversal as it indicates sustained selling pressure and bearish sentiment.
2. **First Candle (Bearish)**: The first candle in the pattern must be bearish, signifying that sellers were still in control at the beginning of the pattern. This candle typically has a smaller body compared to the second candle.
3. **Second Candle (Bullish)**: The second candle is a bullish candle that completely engulfs the body of the first candle. This means the opening price of the second candle is lower than the close of the first candle, and the close of the second candle is higher than the opening of the first candle. The larger bullish candle demonstrates that buyers have overwhelmed the sellers, reversing the bearish momentum.
4. **No Shadows Overlapping**: Ideally, the bodies of the candles should not have overlapping shadows, although this is not a strict requirement. The emphasis is on the bodies of the candles, with the second candle's body fully engulfing the first candle's body.

Why the Bullish Engulfing Pattern Works

The Bullish Engulfing pattern is believed by most traders to be a strong reversal pattern. Due to its dramatic shift in market sentiment, the pattern suggests that after a prolonged period of selling (downtrend), a surge of buying emerges, overpowering the sellers. The first bearish candle signals the continuation of the downtrend, indicating that sellers are still in control. However, the second bullish candle is a strong countermeasure by the buyers who absorb the selling pressure and further push it to the upside, thus turning around a bearish move.

Now that traders have been essentially 'shaken out', a sudden shift in sentiment may happen, causing buying interest to skyrocket as market participants recognise the reversal signal. The larger, more bullish candle in the pattern signals to the market that buyers are now fully back in charge, and this can spark further buying, moving into a larger upward trend.

Trading the Bullish Engulfing Pattern

To effectively trade the Bullish Engulfing pattern, traders should consider the following strategies:

1. **Confirmation**: While the Bullish Engulfing pattern is a strong reversal signal, waiting for confirmation can reduce the risk of false signals. Confirmation typically comes in the form of continued buying pressure and a higher close on the day following the engulfing pattern. This further validates the strength of the bullish reversal.

2. **Volume Analysis**: Analysing volume can enhance the reliability of the Bullish Engulfing pattern. A significant increase in volume on the day of the Bullish Engulfing candle indicates strong buying interest and reinforces the likelihood of a sustained reversal.

3. **Support Levels**: The effectiveness of the Bullish Engulfing pattern can be enhanced when it forms near key support levels. Support levels are areas where buying interest is historically strong, making a reversal more likely. Traders should look for confluence between the pattern and support levels to increase the probability of a successful trade.

4. **Risk Management**: As with any trading strategy, risk management is crucial. Setting stop-loss orders below the low of the Bullish Engulfing candle can help protect against unexpected market moves. Additionally, traders should consider their risk-reward ratio and position size to ensure that they are not overexposed to any single trade.

The Bullish Engulfing pattern provides traders with a significant two-day reversal signal that can help turn the tides in favour of a potential market reversal. With the information about how this pattern is created and what it means, traders can successfully identify and trade a bullish reversal. The secret to success is to wait for a confirmation, analyse volume and support levels and implement risk management. Traders can enhance their ability to gauge market trends accurately and capitalise on profit opportunities by making use of the Bullish Engulfing trading model.

Bearish Engulfing Pattern

Now, let's delve into the Bearish Engulfing pattern, another powerful reversal signal in candlestick charting. This pattern, like its bullish counterpart, belongs to the two-day reversal patterns and signals a potential shift from an uptrend to a downtrend.

In this case, we see a Bearish Engulfing pattern that is formed by a smaller bullish/white candlestick, and a next immediate bigger bearish/black candlestick that completely closes below the low of the previous one.

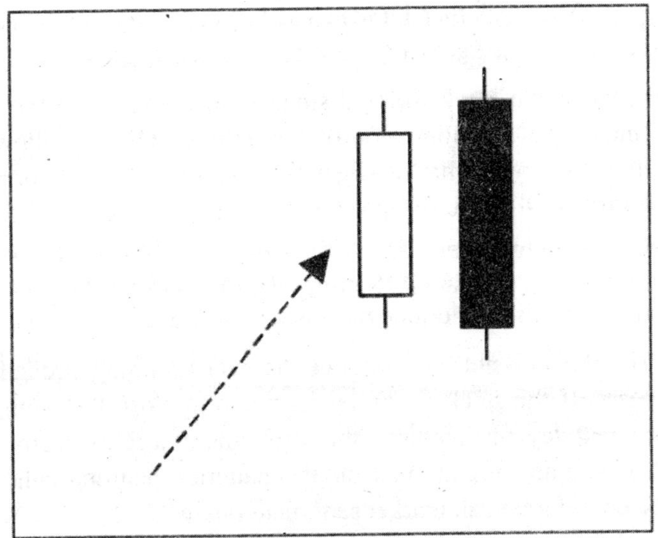

Bearish Engulfing signal

Criteria for Validity

To validate the Bearish Engulfing pattern, we need to have these conditions below:

1. **Uptrend Before the Signal**: The stock should have been in an uptrend leading up to the appearance of the Bearish Engulfing pattern. This trend is very clearly shown on the chart.

2. **Engulfing Black Candle**: A black (bearish) candle must completely engulf the prior white (bullish) candle in the following trading day. If a Doji appears after the first bullish candle and is followed by a Bearish Engulfing candle, it can strengthen the bearish candle.

Why the Reversal Works: Imagine a stock that has been steadily rising, reaching all-time highs every day, and where the investors are smiling while watching their gains every day. These investors get more confident as they expect the stock to keep going up. The stock then builds up selling pressure when it finally reaches a key value area after several consistent gains.

Initially, the stock forms a small bullish candle on the first day, indicating a continuation of the uptrend. On the following day, the stock opens flat or slightly up but encounters a surge in selling pressure as the day progresses. This can lead to increased volatility and downward movement in the near term. This sudden about-turn suggests that the bears are in control here, and any remaining bullish undertone has lost all its strength.

The bulls do not fail to notice the overwhelming strength of the bears. If the stock continues its move to close lower on the subsequent day, this confirms the beginning of a reversal from an uptrend to a downtrend. As such, this pattern is a strong indicator of the end of a bullish market sentiment phase.

Enhancing the Signal's Strength

While the Bearish Engulfing pattern is strong on its own, the following conditions can increase the likelihood of a successful trend reversal:

1. **Long Bullish Candle**: The body of the first day's bullish candle is relatively long compared to other candles in the current uptrend. This underscores the strength of the bulls before the reversal.
2. **Volume Spike**: A noticeable increase in volume on either of the two signal days adds credibility to the pattern. High volume indicates strong participation by traders and reinforces the likelihood of a bearish reversal.
3. **Gap Up**: The initial bullish candle gaps up from the previous trend, showing exuberance and confidence among the bulls. The subsequent engulfing by a bearish candle highlights a dramatic shift in sentiment.

4. **Overbought Stochastics**: Stochastic indicators in overbought conditions suggest that the stock has been overextended and is due for a correction. This condition aligns with the bearish reversal indicated by the pattern.
5. **Multiple Candles Engulfed**: If the second day's bearish candle engulfs more than one bullish candle from the previous trend, it strengthens the signal, indicating a more decisive shift in market sentiment.

Practical Application

For those of you who are aiming to catch a potential reversal, it is vital to know how a Bearish Engulfing pattern works. Understanding this pattern allows traders to identify shifts in market sentiment. By integrating this pattern with technical analysis tools, traders can make informed decisions when entering or exiting trades. This signals not only a trend reversal but also highlights the market psychology that can fuel massive price movements when confidence collapses into fear.

To simplify this, if a trader sees a Bearish Engulfing forming, they should confirm the same on the following trading day. If the stock continues to move lower, then it is a good indicator that somebody is considering either bailing on longs or even going short. In addition to volume spikes, gaps and Stochastic Oscillators can be observed to confirm the strength of the reversal and improve your trading odds.

Bottom Line

The Bearish Engulfing signal is useful for traders. By learning how an engulfing pattern occurs, its parameters, and the market psychology behind it, traders benefit from knowing what to look for in trading signals and are better equipped to adapt their strategies as part of their trading plan.

The Bearish and Bullish Engulfing candlestick patterns signify prominent signals for traders as they can signal market trend reversals. Consisting of two candles, these patterns see the body of the second candle engulfing the body of the first entirely, setting an indication of the change in market sentiment.

Engulfing Patterns

Traders can trade based on engulfing patterns as it provides more information to the trader than just directional movement. If you see a Bullish Engulfing pattern as the price bottoms during a downtrend, it could be an indication that the supply has dried up and buyers are showing interest. Such an occurrence might indicate a signal to traders to enter into long positions on the asset, expecting a price reversal.

Similarly, a Bearish Engulfing pattern at the end of an uptrend implies a reversal to the downside. Traders who recognise this formation may then wish to sell or short the asset, anticipating a price drop.

Traders should not blindly follow candlestick formations such as engulfing patterns, but verify them with other indicators or techniques to confirm their trade ideas. In addition to this, you should also take into account the general market environment and news events that may affect the price of the asset in one direction or another.

That wraps up engulfing candlestick patterns and how traders use these to find them and execute a potential market reversal. Traders can use this knowledge to improve the precision of their trades.

But beware there's an exception as well

If the engulfing pattern does not behave as expected, then it is conditioned by the presence of specific market conditions. A good example of this is if a Bullish Engulfing pattern forms in an area where the market is already overbought. In such a scenario, the bullish signal can essentially have a bearish implication—a phenomenon known as last-gasp buying.

This is a sound strategy if correctly implemented. However, novice investors may perceive this gap down in the stock price during an overbought market as a buying opportunity. They may be eager to join the market that is raging, driven by the fear of missing potential gains. Their entry can temporarily inflate the price, making it look like a Bullish Engulfing pattern. But this price bounce is typically a trap, as institutional investors are distributing their coins.

In such conditions, the Bullish Engulfing pattern serves as a precursor indicating a possible change of trend. It's a foreshadow that tells the market sentiment is changing, and the ongoing uptrend may be nearing its trend. Recognising these anomalies and incorporating them into the broader market analysis scheme can help traders avoid pitfalls and help them make more informed trading decisions.

Any serious trader can benefit significantly from understanding and correctly utilising the signals sent by the candlestick patterns. Beyond simply recognising when to expect these patterns, learning the psychology behind these signals can reveal nuanced insights into the functioning of the market.

If a Bearish Engulfing signal occurs in an oversold area, it signifies bullish implications. The smart money behind these very large orders may begin buying during such extended downtrends. This increased buying pressure causes a gap up in prices, prompting retail traders to perceive it as an opportunity to offload their shares. This dynamic briefly forms the Bearish Engulfing pattern. Ultimately, when smart money collectively opposes a price direction, it tends to overpower it, despite occasional setbacks due to herd behaviour.

Mastering candlestick signals can lead to significant gains, as proven over time. Gradually, traders can learn to read charts and analyse them based on two simple facts relevant to the underlying security.

If a candlestick sell signal occurs in an overbought condition, it must be followed with more selling to confirm that sellers are active.

Conversely, if a candlestick signals a buy signal in an oversold condition, it must be accompanied by confirmed buying to prove that the buyers are serious about reversing the trend.

Although these principles may appear to be common sense, they are key to trading success and can make or break a trader in the market.

❑

5

Dark Cloud Cover and Piercing Line

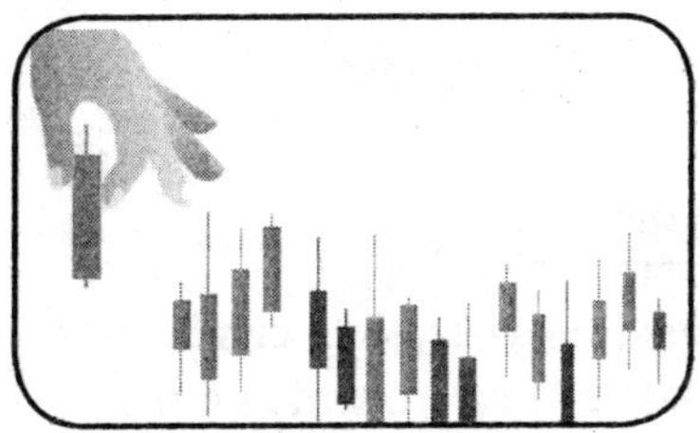

The Dark Cloud Cover and Piercing Line signals are both intermediate indicators of market reversals. Even though they resemble the Bearish Engulfing and Bullish Engulfing patterns, they are nowhere near as strong or definitive.

The Dark Cloud Cover pattern occurs during an uptrend with a white (or green) candle body followed by a black candle with a smaller body, which opens above the close of the previous candle but closes below its midpoint. This pattern is considered a reversal pattern from uptrend to downtrend. Although not as powerful as the Bearish Engulfing signal, it is a signal that the momentum may be changing.

Conversely, the Piercing Line pattern occurs exclusively in a bearish trend and requires a white (green) candle after a black (red) one to open below the previous day's close and close higher than the midpoint of the body of the same day. This pattern indicates that an existing downtrend might reverse itself and become an uptrend. Although the Bullish Engulfing pattern is a stronger signal, the Cloud Cover and Piercing Line compel attention by signalling a change in investor sentiment.

This pattern is not as reliable as the engulfing patterns so traders should be careful when dealing with them. It can be beneficial to use other technical indicators or candlestick patterns to confirm these signals before making the trade.

Let's understand them in detail now.

The Piercing Signal

The Piercing Signal is a classic candlestick pattern that can indicate a potential reversal in a downtrend. This signal forms when a white candle opens below the low of the previous day's trading range but closes above the midpoint of the previous day's dark body. Visually, it appears as a white candle that pierces through the dark candle from the previous day, hence the name 'Piercing Signal'.

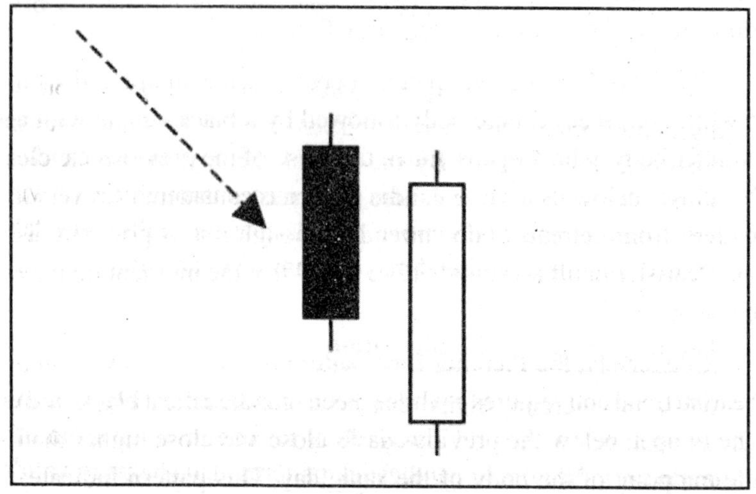

Piercing Signal

Criteria for a Valid Piercing Signal

For a Piercing Signal to be considered valid, the following conditions must exist:

1. The stock must have been in a definite downtrend before this signal occurred, which can be visually observed on the chart.
2. The second day of the signal should be a white candle that opens below the trading range of the previous day and closes at least halfway into the body of the previous day's dark candle.

The Psychology Behind the Reversal

The formation of a Piercing Signal reflects a shift in market sentiment from bearish to bullish. Let's consider an example with a stock, XYZ, that has been steadily declining. As the stock continues to drop, investors holding the stock start to lose confidence and may begin to sell, contributing to a significant sell-off. This sell-off often leads to a gap down in the stock's price, indicating high selling pressure.

However, smart investors see this as an opportunity to buy at a discounted price. They step in and start buying the shares, causing the stock price to rise. By the end of the day, the stock closes higher, forming a white candle that pierces through the previous day's dark candle. This move signals that the bulls have taken control, and the downtrend may be coming to an end.

The Importance of Confirmation

While the Piercing Signal can be a strong indication of a trend reversal, traders should always look for confirmation from other technical indicators or candlestick patterns. This helps to validate the signal and reduce the risk of false signals. Some additional conditions that can confirm a trend reversal include:

1. The first day's dark candle body is significantly longer compared to other candles in the recent downtrend.
2. There is a spike in trading volume on either of the two signal days, indicating increased buying interest.
3. The first dark candle gaps down from the previous trend, suggesting panic selling.
4. The Stochastic Oscillator is in an oversold condition, indicating that the stock may be due for a bounce.

The Piercing Signal is a valuable tool for traders looking to identify potential trend reversals. However, it is essential to use this signal in conjunction with other technical analysis tools to confirm the reversal and make informed trading decisions.

The Dark Cloud Cover

The Dark Cloud Cover is a candlestick pattern that may signify a potential reversal during an uptrend. This occurs when during

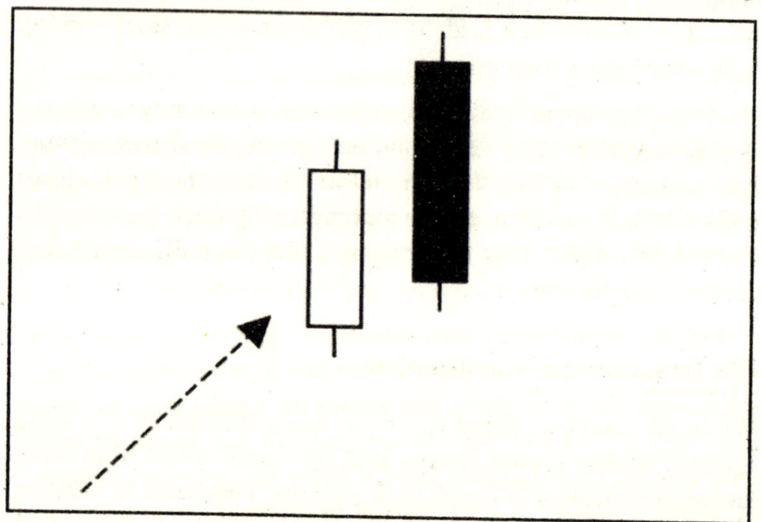

Dark Cloud Cover signal

an uptrend, a black (or dark) candle opens above the high of the trading range from the previous day; however, its closing is below the midpoint of the previous white (or preferably, bullish) candlestick. This forms a visual pattern that looks like a dark cloud covering the bullish candle from the previous day, hence the name 'Dark Cloud Cover'.

Criteria for a Valid Dark Cloud Cover Signal

For a Dark Cloud Cover signal to be considered valid, the following conditions must exist:

1. The stock must have been in a definite uptrend before this signal occurs, which can be visually verified on the chart.
2. On the second day of the signal, the candle should open above the previous white candle's trading range and close more than halfway into it, forming a black body.

The Psychology Behind the Reversal

The Dark Cloud Cover pattern appears at the end of bullish trends and foretells potential bearish reversals from a place of resistance. Here's an example of a stock that has been trending higher. The stock experiences a substantial increase, which leads to a massive white candle as the investors are excited. The price gaps up on the next day, which may lead novice traders to believe that the uptrend will continue.

But the smart money uses that as an opportunity to sell at a higher price. This prompts them to liquidate their current positions, which sends the price down and causes the candle stick to close more than 50% below the closing price of the previous day's white candle. This suggests that the bears are growing stronger, potentially signalling a weakening of the uptrend.

The Importance of Confirmation

As with any candlestick pattern, it is crucial to seek confirmation from other technical indicators or patterns before making a trading decision. Some additional conditions that can confirm a trend reversal when combined with the Dark Cloud Cover pattern include:

1. The first day's white candle body is significantly longer compared to other candles in the recent uptrend.
2. There is a spike in trading volume on either of the two signal days, indicating increased selling pressure.
3. The first white candle has gapped up from the previous trend, showing excessive optimism among traders.
4. The stochastics are in an overbought condition, suggesting that the stock may be due for a pullback.

The Dark Cloud Cover pattern is a valuable tool for traders looking to identify potential trend reversals. However, it is essential to use this pattern in conjunction with other technical analysis tools to confirm the reversal and make informed trading decisions.

Candlestick patterns like the Dark Cloud Cover or Piercing Line show traders how to make informed investments in the markets. The patterns can give you an indication of when a trend is turning, which is very useful for knowing when to place a trade or close one. Appreciating these patterns, and how they should be interpreted will vastly improve a trader's ability to execute wise trades within the marketplace.

The Dark Cloud Cover and Piercing Line are both two-day reversal patterns that indicate a likely change in the stock's trend direction in a two-day span. The Dark Cloud Cover appears in an uptrend and signals a bearish reversal, while the Piercing Line appears in a downtrend and signals a bullish reversal. Traders who can identify these patterns early can profit from subsequent price moves.

Here is an example that highlights the importance of these signals. For example, let us say that a trader has been analysing the price action of a stock that has been trending upward for a few weeks. The stock is in a bullish phase, and the trader is planning to enter a long trade on the next higher high, anticipating another momentum-driven move.

One day, a day trader sees a Dark Cloud Cover Japanese candlestick pattern appearing on the daily chart. Initially, the chart shows a large white (bullish) candle, with an opening gap, indicating continued buying pressure. However, on the following day, the stock gaps higher at the open but closes significantly lower, forming a dark (bearish) candlestick that engulfs more than half of the previous day's white real body. This pattern suggests that the upward momentum may be waning and potentially reversing.

Meanwhile, the trader also notes that the stock is showing overbought signs on the Stochastic Oscillator, potentially signalling that the stock could be in for a drop. Moreover, the second day of this pattern demonstrates a substantial uptick in volume that helps to validate the bearishness.

After analysing this, the trader decides to short the market expecting the price to drop. The stock price naturally then proceeds to fall in the following days, confirming the occurrence of the Dark Cloud Cover pattern. This allows the trader to profit from the reversal, subsequently exiting the transaction at a favourable price.

In the same way, traders can take advantage of an emerging uptrend by going long at the very beginning, at the breakout point.

To summarise all the points we have discussed above, monitoring candlestick patterns like the Dark Cloud Cover and Piercing Line can be a beneficial practice for traders to forecast trend reversals in advance and make informed trading decisions. Through an awareness of these patterns, traders may use them to increase the likelihood of success in the market by incorporating them with other technical analysis tools.

As a candlestick trader, you will begin to look at the market not just as price movement along a scale of time, but rather through human emotions, specifically fear and greed. Those emotions are what create patterns on a price chart and drive the buying and selling decisions of traders. By recognising these patterns, you get an insight into the psychology of other market participants and profit from it.

For instance, a Dark Cloud Cover pattern will show you the moment investors go from being bullish to becoming bearish. Day one opened with a gap up and rallied which reflects the greed among traders, pushing prices higher without being supported by fundamental factors driving the market. But the reversal on day two is a clue that all this optimism may be unfounded, for sellers have gained control and brought the price sharply downwards. Once you see this type of pattern emerging, you can expect a downturn and adjust your trading strategy accordingly.

The same is the case when you notice a Piercing Line pattern, which signifies a transition from fear to hope. The first day opens with a gap down, indicating the fear and panic of sellers in a hurry to exit positions. The rally on the second day is a suggestion that the trend will reverse as buyers come back into play and start to push prices higher. If you see this pattern, it means that the current downtrend may be nearing completion for you to prepare to BUY and collect profits from the expected uptrend.

Keep in mind that these candlestick patterns are time-tested as they have been used by Japanese traders for centuries. Their historical use is a strong testament to their reliability and effectiveness. By training yourself to recognise and interpret candlestick patterns, you will be in a better position to cultivate winning trading decisions and raise your odds of profitability in trading.

So in summary, view the market through the lens of human emotions and train yourself to recognise patterns and identify shifts in market trends. With a firm grasp of the patterns and the psychology behind them, traders are better equipped with the ability to read market trends more accurately.

❑

6

The Harami Pattern

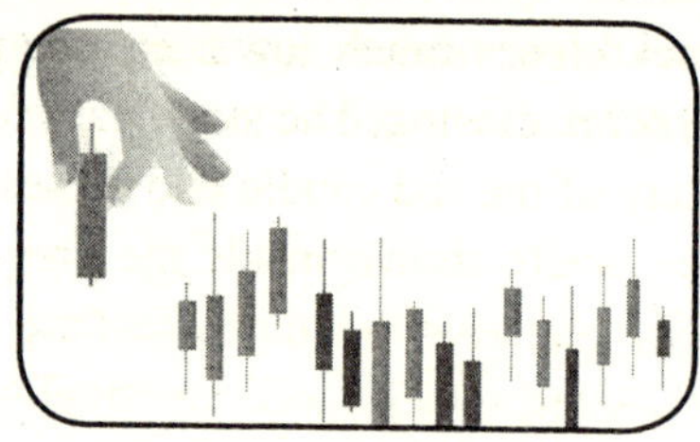

The Harami Pattern

The Harami is a major reversal candlestick pattern; it is recognised by many as a sign of possible market changes. The name 'Harami' derived from Japanese translates to 'pregnant', depicting the pattern's appearance resembling a pregnant woman. The Harami pattern consists of two candlesticks: The first candlestick which is large and the second smaller candlestick which appears within the range of the first candlestick, resembling a pregnant woman's belly.

Harami Candlestick Definition

The Harami is crucial in predicting reversals in the market trend. The Harami denotes that the current trend—either bullish or bearish—is losing steam and a potential reversal might be around the corner.

Bullish Harami

The first day shows a big bearish candle where sellers were clearly the dominant party. A small bullish candle is formed within the body of the first day's candle on the second day. This smaller candle symbolises indecision by the traders. This implies that the sellers are running out of steam and the buyers might be back in control.

For example, think about a stock that has seen a constant downtrend. The stock closes much lower on one particular day with a big red candlestick closing. The stock gaps up the next day and opens in the body of the red candle and closes higher which forms a small green candle shown inside the previous day's red candle. This formation suggests that the sellers are exhausted and the buyers are taking over, which could eventually mark the end of a downtrend and the start of an uptrend.

How to spot a Bullish Harami: First confirm if the stock is in a downtrend. The pattern consists of two candles—a larger-sized dark candle followed by a light smaller candle. The second candle's body must be fully engulfed within the body of the first, larger candle. The tails (wicks) of the smaller candle do not need to be engulfed by the larger candle as well.

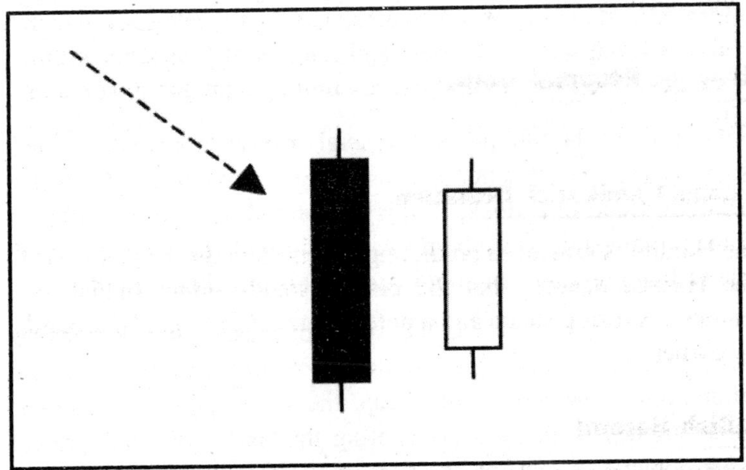

Bullish Harami signal

Understanding the Bullish Harami

The Bullish Harami pattern signals a potential reversal in a downtrend. It appears as a smaller white (or light-coloured) candle completely engulfed by the previous day's larger black (or dark-coloured) candle. This pattern suggests a shift in market sentiment from bearish to bullish.

Criteria for a Valid Bullish Harami

For a Bullish Harami signal to be considered valid, several conditions must be met:

Definite Downtrend: The stock must have been in a clear downtrend before this signal appeared. This can be visually confirmed on the chart, where the stock price shows a series of lower highs and lower lows.

Engulfing Pattern: The second day's candle should be white, and its body should be entirely engulfed by the previous day's black candle body. The size of the wicks is less important than the body itself.

Why the Reversal Works

The Bullish Harami plays a crucial role as a reversal signal showing that market sentiment has changed dramatically. Consider a falling trend in a stock. In this downtrend, novice investors or traders may panic at the bottom and contribute to the intensity of the selling pressure that culminates in this long black candle.

However, demand for the stock increases, due perhaps to some positive news or a resumption of optimism among investors after hours. The next trading day, the stock gaps up, allowing smart money to begin accumulating the shares at lower prices. This demand is seen by the formation of a small white candle inside the larger black candle body. This causes the sellers (bears) to get uncomfortable. Those who had shorted the stock hoping that it would plunge further began getting second thoughts. They then wait to see if that bullishness will continue into the next day.

On the third day, as the stock climbs higher again, those who hold short positions begin to buy back the shares they short sold, contributing to upward pressure on the stock. Therefore the bulls get encouraged and the uptrend gains momentum.

Enhancing the Bullish Harami Signal

Several factors can strengthen the Bullish Harami signal, making it a more compelling buy opportunity:

Length of Candles: The longer the black engulfing candle and the white engulfed candle, the higher the likelihood of a trend reversal. A significant difference in candle lengths indicates a substantial shift in market sentiment.

Volume: Heavy trading volume on either of the two days of the signal formation can add credibility to the pattern. High volume suggests strong participation by traders, which is necessary for a sustainable reversal.

Oversold Condition: If the stock is in an oversold condition, indicated by technical indicators such as the Stochastic Oscillator, the Bullish Harami becomes more convincing. An oversold condition implies that the stock has been excessively sold and is due for a rebound.

Closing Price: The higher the white candle closes into the black candle body, the greater the probability of a reversal. A strong close indicates that buyers are willing to pay higher prices, reinforcing the bullish sentiment.

Example of Bullish Harami Pattern: XYZ has been in a consistent downtrend for several weeks and you short it. The price has been making lower highs and lower lows which shows consistent selling pressure on the stock. During a particularly volatile session, the stock market experiences a significant downturn, resulting in the stock forming a large black candlestick. This long black candle sums up the selling pressure and panic of many inexperienced traders.

On the following day, the stock opens higher above the previous day's close after positive earnings reports or a rosy economic outlook. The stock price continues to rise higher over the course of the day, creating a smaller-sized white candlestick entirely within the previous day's black body. As soon as the trader recognises this Bullish Harami pattern, he intends to wait for more information on day three.

If the stock can break higher on day three, this confirms the reversal signal. At this stage, the trader might choose to go long, hoping the share price will move higher. This reinforces the Bullish Harami confirmation along with strong trading volume and oversold conditions, ensuring a valid trade.

Bearish Harami

On the contrary, in an uptrend context appears a Bearish Harami. The stock has been trending upwards, characterised by higher highs and higher lows. During a particularly bullish session, the stock posts a very large bullish candle, showing the buyers are alive and well. On the second day, a bearish candle is formed within the body of the previous day's candle. The smaller candle indicates that buyers

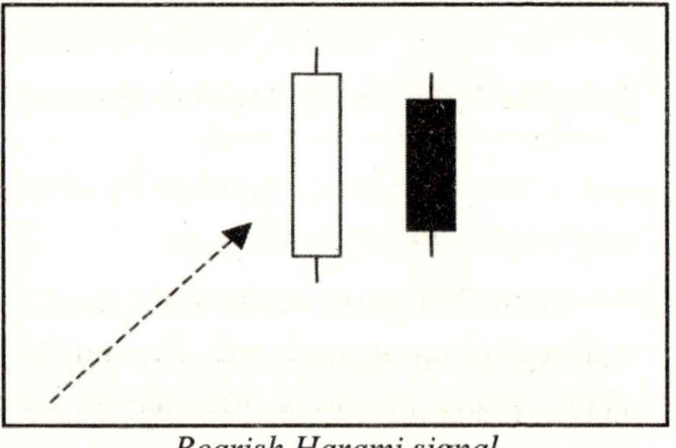

Bearish Harami signal

are losing momentum and we may see the sellers flexing their muscles.

To see exactly what I mean, let's start with an example of a stock that has been trending up nicely for a while. After a significant rally day, the stock closes much higher making a large green candlestick. The next day, the stock opens within the body of the previous day's candle and closes down, creating a small red candle inside the green candle. This means that the excitement of traders to buy has waned as sellers become aggressive, signalling that this is the end of the uptrend and marks the start of a downtrend.

The Bearish Harami is a two-day bearish reversal pattern of great significance in candlestick charts with the potential to signal a shift from an uptrend to a downtrend. The pattern is a large and white (or light) candle followed by a small and black (or dark) candle. While it's not mandatory for the smaller candle's wicks (tail) to be within the previous candle's range, the smaller candle should be contained within the larger candle's body.

Understanding the Bearish Harami

The Bearish Harami pattern suggests a shift in market sentiment from bullish to bearish. The formation starts with a large white candle, followed by a smaller black candle whose body is entirely within the range of the previous candle's body.

Criteria for a Valid Bearish Harami

For a Bearish Harami signal to be considered valid, the following conditions must be met:

Definite Uptrend: The stock must have been in a clear uptrend before this signal appeared. This can be visually confirmed on the chart, where the stock price shows a series of higher highs and higher lows.

Engulfing Pattern: The second day's candle should be black, and its body should be entirely engulfed by the previous day's white candle body. The size of the wicks is less important than the body itself.

Why the Reversal Works

The Bearish Harami works as a reversal signal because it suggests a strong shift in investor sentiment. Imagine a stock that has been trending up. A large white candle is caused when new investors or traders become bullish near the peak. This is a buying climax.

However, the stock becomes less desirable to own, because of some negative news or a shift in perception of the market after trading hours. The next day the stock gaps down and smart money begins selling. The increased selling pressure creates a small black candle formed within the body of the previous white one. This Bearish Harami pattern is unwelcome news for bulls. Traders who recently entered the stock, expecting continued upward momentum, begin to question their buy. They wait anxiously to see if the bearish momentum will continue into the next trading session.

On the third day, if the stock continues its decline, it confirms the reversal signal. This is a critical moment when traders who recently bought the stock start selling (due to fear) creating even more downward pressure. Once the bulls (buyers) start selling, the bears (sellers) shorting the stock continue to provide downward momentum. Consequently, the trend changes to down and a new decline starts.

Enhancing the Bearish Harami Signal

Several factors can strengthen the Bearish Harami signal, making it a more compelling short-selling opportunity:

Length of Candles: The longer the white engulfing candle and the black engulfed candle, the higher the likelihood of a trend reversal. A significant difference in candle lengths indicates a substantial shift in market sentiment.

Volume: Heavy trading volume on either of the two days of the signal formation can add credibility to the pattern. High volume suggests strong participation by traders, which is necessary for a sustainable reversal.

Overbought Condition: If the stock is in an overbought condition, indicated by technical indicators such as the Stochastic Oscillator, the Bearish Harami becomes more convincing. An overbought condition implies that the stock has been excessively bought and is due for a correction.

Closing Price: The deeper the black candle closes into the white candle's body, the greater the probability of a reversal. A strong close indicates that sellers are willing to sell at lower prices, reinforcing the bearish sentiment.

Practical Example

A practical example to illustrate the Bearish Harami pattern: Consider XYZ stock which has been rising consistently for many weeks. The stock is consistently making higher highs and higher lows, which means continuous buying interest. The stock is significantly higher and forms a large white candle. This pattern marks the start of the Bullish Engulfing reversal pattern. This long white candle was born as a representation of bullish momentum, and the euphoria generated among amateur traders.

However, the following day, the stock gaps down on lacklustre earnings or economic indicators. The stock falls further throughout the day and forms a small black candle that fits entirely within the body of the previous day's white candle. The trader waits on the confirmation of the Bearish Harami pattern.

If on the third day, the stock makes a new lower low close, the bearish reversal has been confirmed from this 'three inside down' candlestick pattern. The trader might then decide to go short, expecting the stock price to fall. The Bearish Harami pattern is confirmed and reinforced by high trading volume and an overbought condition.

The Psychology Behind the Harami Pattern

The Harami is a candlestick pattern rooted in market psychology, offering insights into shifts in trader sentiment. During a downtrend, the Bullish Harami begins with a large bearish candle representing dominance by sellers in the market. The smaller bullish candle on the following day indicates that the sellers are no longer so strong and buyers are beginning to take initiative. This change in sentiment indicates that the bear market could be playing out its final act.

During an uptrend, the first day of the Bearish Harami is a large bullish candle that displays powerful buying interest. The smaller bearish daily candle within the previous day's range depicts that the buyers are losing momentum and the sellers are taking over. The change in sentiment now indicates a reversal or pause in the uptrend.

Trading the Harami Pattern and Confirmation

The Harami pattern is a strong reversal signal. However, it is advised to wait for confirmation before you take any trade. And we get our confirmation on the next bar! A higher close is possible or a gap up opening on the third day would validate the Bullish Harami. Conversely, in the case of a Bearish Harami, traders would look for a lower close on the third day, signalling an increase in selling pressure and potential reversal.

Practical Example

Let's consider an example to illustrate the Harami pattern. Imagine a trader monitoring a stock that has been in a pronounced downtrend for weeks, consistently forming lower highs and lower lows. One day, the stock drops significantly, closing much lower, creating a big red candle stick. This candle opens within the body of the previous day. On the following day, the stock opens within the previous day's range and closes higher, forming a smaller green candlestick within the previous day's red body. The trader notices this Bullish Harami and waits for it to play out on the third day. If the stock continues to and closes above the highs of the previous days, a buying opportunity may be imminent.

Conversely, during an uptrend, imagine a trader observing a stock that has been rising steadily. A few days later, the stock closed at its highest price so far with a large green candle. On the following day, the stock opens within the body of the previous day's green candle and closes lower. Upon seeing this pattern on the first two days, the trader waits for confirmation on the third day. If the stock makes a lower close on the third day, the trader may consider taking a short position based on the expectation of a due reversal and selling off in the stock price.

The Harami pattern is one of the most powerful weapons in a trader's arsenal and if understood properly, can provide us with many profitable insights into upcoming market reversals. By learning the psychology behind the pattern and waiting for confirmation, traders can increase the likelihood of profitable trades. Whether trading indices, forex or soft commodities, incorporating the Harami pattern into your trading plan can prove beneficial.

Practicing and being patient is crucial to effectively integrate the Harami pattern into your list of trading strategies. Like any trading strategy, you should incorporate technical analysis along with stringent risk control techniques. In this way, you will get confirmation of the Harami pattern that will build your trust and help you in placing trades which are mostly likely to be market reversals.

The Importance of Monitoring Harami Formations for Traders

For traders, mastering candlestick patterns is incredibly important, as it helps you to make informed decisions that can maximise profits. The Harami formation is one of the most important patterns to recognise. Both Bullish and Bearish Harami patterns provide early indications of potential trend reversals, making it a valuable tool in a trader's arsenal. Here's why it is essential to keep an eye on Harami formations.

Early Reversal Signals

The Harami pattern is a two-day reversal signal that might indicate a change in the market sentiment. If a Bullish Harami forms following a protracted price decline, it serves to hint that the selling pressure is beginning to wane and that an investor may perceive a potential bottom. If the Bearish Harami forms after an uptrend, this could suggest that buying pressure is weakening and a downtrend may start. Early recognition of these patterns enables traders to position themselves favourably in anticipation of a trend reversal.

Psychological Insights

Smart trading hinges on understanding the psychology of Japanese candlestick patterns, including the Harami trend reversal pattern. A Harami pattern signifies indecision in the market. Take, for example, the first long black candle in a Bullish Harami that suggests strong selling pressure. However, the subsequent small white candlestick which is engulfed within the real body of the prior day's candle suggests that the sellers are losing control and buyers are stepping in. Knowing this change in psychology can be a great help for traders to read market sentiment and execute better trading decisions.

Confirmation of Market Conditions

In particular, a genuine Harami pattern identifies a specific state of the market. In order to have a Bullish Harami, the stock has to be in a clear downtrend, indicating a pause in downward momentum. If it is a Bearish Harami, then the stock must be in an uptrend and the pattern shows a potential reversal in direction. Traders who can spot these conditions are able to confirm signals and thus they can enhance the probability of their forecasts being accurate.

Enhanced Risk Management

Incorporating Harami patterns into a trading strategy can significantly enhance risk management. Traders can use these patterns to identify potential reversals early on. For instance, if a trader sees a Bearish Harami in the context of an uptrend it would indicate that it would be prudent to take profits or place stop-loss orders to guard against a possible downtrend. Similarly, a Bullish Harami in a downtrend can offer traders an opportunity to enter long positions with favourable risk-reward ratios.

Improved Trade Timing

It is also used by traders to fine-tune the timing of their trade entry and exits and is nicknamed the Harami pattern. Trade entry and exit points are crucial for maximising profits and minimising losses. Harami patterns give specific signals to enter or exit a trade, allowing traders to act swiftly. By waiting until the third day to confirm the Harami setup, traders can improve the timing of their entries or minimise whipsaw trades.

Complementary Analysis Tool

The Harami pattern is also a supportive tool, meaning it works well with another technical tool or chart pattern. Use Harami with indicators such as the Relative Strength Index (RSI), Moving Averages or Stochastic Oscillator for a better analysis. For example, a Bullish Harami coupled with an overbought RSI may add assurance to a potential upward reversal, allowing traders to make trades with an added layer of confidence.

Practical Example: Bearish Harami in Action

To illustrate the importance of monitoring Harami formations, let's consider a practical example involving a Bearish Harami pattern.

Consider a stock XYZ, which has been in a strong uptrend for several weeks. The stock had higher highs and higher lows, i.e., consistent buying. One day, the stock closes much higher, showing a long white candle. This long white candle illustrates the height of bullish sentiment.

However, the next day brings unfavourable news and the stock opens lower than the previous day's close (a gap down). The stock trades lower throughout the day, creating a smaller black candle that is entirely contained within the previous day's white candle. The formation is called a Bearish Harami.

Definite Uptrend: Prior to the Bearish Harami, the stock was in a clear uptrend, as visually confirmed on the chart.

Engulfing Pattern: The second day's black candle is completely engulfed by the previous day's white candle body.

Confirmation: Traders wait for confirmation on the third day. If the stock continues to fall and closes lower, it confirms the reversal signal provided by the Bearish Harami.

Recognising the Bearish Harami, traders might take the following actions:

Take Profits: Traders with long positions may choose to take profits, anticipating a potential reversal.

Short Positions: Aggressive traders may enter short positions, betting on the stock's downward movement.

Protective Measures: Traders may place stop-loss orders to protect against potential losses if the stock continues to decline.

Traders must monitor Harami formations as these can provide early reversal signals. Through the identification of these patterns, traders are able to enhance their market analysis, refine trade timing, or manage risks more effectively. Both types of Harami patterns, whether bullish or bearish, offer a significant advantage in the often unpredictable world of financial markets, making this an invaluable tool for traders to plan their trades effectively and stay ahead of market movements. By leveraging the power of Harami patterns, you can enhance your trading and feel more comfortable entering trades.

❑

7

Morning Star and Evening Star

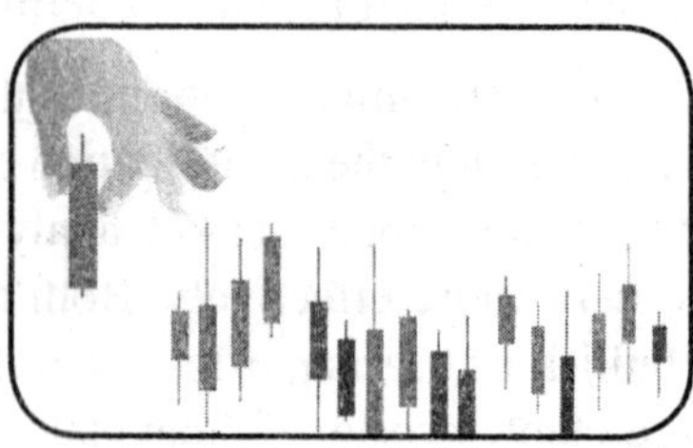

Morning Star and Evening Star Reversal Signals

The Morning Star along with its counterpart, the Evening Star represents one of the most powerful three-day bullish reversal patterns in candlestick charting. When mastered, these patterns can enhance a trader's ability to navigate profitable trades successfully. Understanding these formations is essential for traders looking to capitalise on market opportunities.

Morning Star Pattern

The Morning Star is a bullish reversal pattern and occurs at the bottom of a downtrend. It indicates the possibility of a new uptrend and suggests to traders that they enter long positions.

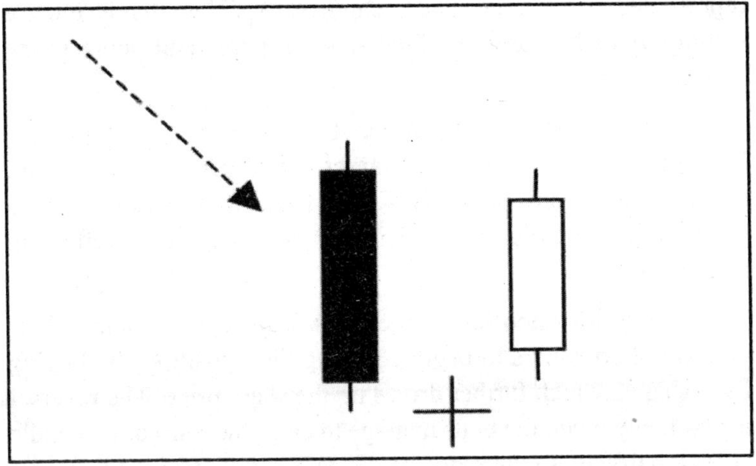

Morning Star signal

Formation and Criteria:

1. **First Candle (Bearish Candle)**: The first day of the pattern features a long bearish candlestick, reflecting a strong downward momentum.
2. **Second Candle (Indecision or Small Candle)**: The second day shows a small candlestick, which can be bullish, bearish, or a Doji. This candle gaps down from the first candle, indicating indecision among traders.
3. **Third Candle (Bullish Candle)**: The third day is characterised by a long bullish candlestick that closes well into the body of the first bearish candle, indicating a strong reversal signal.

Why the Reversal Works

Consider a stock that has been declining steadily over time. Suddenly the investors panic, resulting in a massive sell-off represented by a long black candlestick. This major intense selling typically marks the final stage of panic and doom in the market.

However, the war of bulls and bears begins the following day. Smart money enters the market, while panicked sellers are eager to sell at any price. This tug of war often manifests as a small-bodied candle like a Doji or Spinning Top, reflecting indecision.

Seizing this opportunity, the bulls try to regain control. This prompts short sellers to begin covering their positions by buying back shares, which further drives up the share price. The reversal is valid only when the bulls manage to close the third day's candle at least halfway up the range of the dark candle formed two days earlier. We are now officially in a very high probability trend reversal.

The Morning Star signal is a powerful and visually distinct indicator that signifies a shift in investor sentiment towards a stock. It reveals phases of indecision within the market. When the middle day of the pattern exhibits a one-day reversal signal, it strengthens the Morning Star pattern.

Also, note the bullish Abandoned Baby signal in the same picture. That is a VERY strong reverse signal. Study the formation: observe that there is a gap between the low of the first day and the high of the second day, as well as a gap between the high of the second day and the low of the third every. Let us analyse the fear and greed pattern associated with these formations:

The first gap represents panic selling in the stock. This leads to the bulls and bears fighting for control to be ended on the third day by a bullish move that crushes all opposition. The second gap signifies the strength of the winning trade, including a reversal formation that alerts experienced traders to consider entering the stock at an opportune moment.

Factors Enhancing the Probability of Reversal

Several conditions can enhance the likelihood of a reversal indicated by the Morning Star signal:

1. **Long First Day's Dark Candle**: A long dark candle body on the first day, relative to the overall trading range, signifies intense selling pressure. By the signal's definition, this necessitates that the bullish candle on the third day be large as well, indicating a strong reversal.
2. **Volume Spike on Indecision Day**: A spike in volume on the second day, characterised by patterns such as a Doji or Spinning Top, adds credibility to the pattern. It shows that significant trading activity occurred, reinforcing the importance of the subsequent bullish move.
3. **Oversold Stochastics**: When the stochastics are in an oversold condition, it suggests that the stock has been excessively sold and is due for a reversal. This technical indicator supports the bullish sentiment indicated by the Morning Star pattern.
4. **Middle Day as a One-Day Reversal Signal**: If the second day forms a one-day candlestick reversal pattern, such as a Hammer or a Doji, it strengthens the overall reversal signal. These one-day patterns add further evidence of a potential trend change.

Understanding the psychological fundamentals and technical prerequisites that precede a Morning Star signal could help a trader to identify, analyse and finally confirm reversals in the broader market. Experience in recognising and using this pattern enables traders to clearly discern market action, leading to superior trading decisions that are likely to result in successful outcomes.

Example

Consider a stock XYZ, which has been in a long-term downtrend. The stock concludes one day with a large bearish candle, representing extreme selling pressure. The following day price opens lower and trades between the highs and lows in a small Spinning Top candle. This suggests that sellers are starting to lose control. On the third day, the stock opens at a higher price than the second day but not higher than the close of the first day. This is indicated by a strong white candlestick covering more than half of the range of the first day's black candle. This is a Morning Star, hinting that an uptrend could follow, and it may be time to place long trades.

Evening Star Pattern

The Evening Star is the bearish counterpart to the Morning Star and forms at the end of an uptrend. It is indicative of a potential reversal, signalling the beginning of a downtrend. Traders may interpret it as a signal to consider short positions.

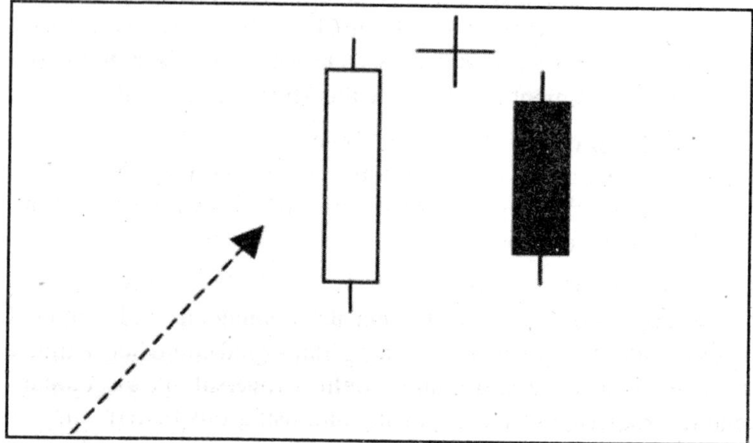

Evening Star signal

Formation and Criteria

1. **First Candle (Bullish Candle)**: The first day of the pattern features a long bullish candlestick, reflecting strong upward momentum.

2. **Second Candle (Indecision or Small Candle)**: The second day shows a small candlestick, which can be bullish, bearish, or a Doji. This candle gaps up from the first candle, indicating indecision among traders.

3. **Third Candle (Bearish Candle)**: The third day is characterised by a long bearish candlestick that closes well into the body of the first bullish candle, indicating a strong reversal signal.

Why the Reversal Works

Novice investors often get excited after an extended rally, jumping on the stock bandwagon. This buying frenzy produces a white candlestick at the top of the uptrend marking the peak of bullish sentiment.

The subsequent day sees a different dynamic; demand from new investors meets supply from sellers. This clash between buyers creates a state of indecision, denoted by a small-bodied candle like the Doji or Spinning Top. These candlestick patterns occur when the forces of buying and selling pressure reach equilibrium, signalling that the rapid spike on the uptrend may be flattening.

The subsequent day sees the bears asserting dominance with a huge downward movement. This third candle is a long black candle, confirming a bearish follow-through, indicating selling pressure overriding buying interest. This pattern marks a potential trend reversal as the bears are reclaiming control from the bulls.

When observing the bearish Abandoned Baby signal, we see gaps between the first and second day, as well as the second and third day which shows a shift in investor sentiment, marking a clear departure from the previous trend. The first gap occurs when buyers have driven the price sharply higher, and the other gap will occur when sellers regain control just as strongly. This swift shift in sentiment highlights the power of the reversal signal. Traders should look to exit long positions and can even consider shorting the index as well to take advantage of a downward move.

Factors Enhancing the Probability of Reversal

Several factors can enhance the likelihood of a reversal indicated by the Evening Star signal:

1. **Long First Day's White Candle**: A long white candle body on the first day, compared to the recent trading range, signifies strong buying pressure and exuberant buying. This over-enthusiasm often precedes a reversal, making the subsequent bearish movement more significant.
2. **Volume Spike on Indecision Day**: A spike in volume on the second day, which represents indecision, adds credibility to the pattern. It shows that significant trading activity occurred, reinforcing the importance of the subsequent bearish move.
3. **Overbought Stochastics**: When the stochastics are in an overbought condition, it suggests that the stock has been excessively bought and is due for a correction. This technical indicator supports the bearish sentiment indicated by the Evening Star pattern.

Example

Consider a tech stock that has been rallying hard for several weeks, becoming the favourite of retail investors. There is a final surge to the upside resulting in a long white candle on the first day of the pattern. This candle signifies peak investor optimism and buying pressure.

The following day, it opens slightly higher but fails to continue the upward momentum, resulting in a Doji (small-bodied candle) where the opening and closing prices are nearly the same. This ambivalence signals that the buyers and sellers are evenly matched in power. The smart money is selling into the strength and taking profit, while the novice retail investor who was late to the party has no idea what to do next.

On day three, the stock opens with a downward gap and continues to decline, forming a long dark candle. This action signals that the bears are now in charge and the earlier trend appears to be likely to be coming to an end. Notice the Evening Star pattern forming, which provides a very solid signal for traders to not only liquidate long positions but possibly even initiate short positions, anticipating further price decline.

Part of the essential knowledge in any trader's toolkit is knowing and recognising candlestick patterns such as the Harami and Star formations. These patterns serve as crucial signals of market sentiment and potential reversals, allowing the trader to act on information advantages. Having said this, the Morning Star and Evening Star patterns specifically provide pivotal reversal signals that can lead to trading opportunities.

Understanding these patterns and recognising their profitability potential allows traders to effectively identify trends, minimise risks, and enhance the likelihood of a successful trading portfolio. Whether new to trading or seasoned, mastering these patterns enables traders to interpret the market efficiently and make informed decisions when anticipating trend reversals.

Imagine there is a stock, ABC, that has been steadily moving up. The stock closes with a long bullish candlestick, indicating the strong buying pressure on the first day. The stock then gaps up the following day and trades in a narrow range, which forms a small Doji. This means that the buyers are losing power. After a few days, on the third day of the triangle, the stocks open lower and continue on a bearish note, forming a strong bearish candlestick that engulfs more than half of the first day's bullish candle. This pattern resembles an Evening Star, which is a strong signal for traders to initiate short positions.

Importance of Monitoring Star Formations

It is crucial for traders to keep an eye on pattern formations such as the Morning Star or Evening Star. They provide indications that a reversal may be imminent, based on the psychological behaviours of market participants observed over centuries of market history.

Practical Applications and Benefits

1. **Early Reversal Detection**: Both the Morning Star and Evening Star patterns provide early indications of potential trend reversals, allowing traders to enter or exit positions ahead of significant market moves.
2. **Enhanced Trade Timing**: By recognising these patterns, traders can improve the timing of their trades, entering long positions at the start of an uptrend or short positions at the start of a downtrend.
3. **Risk Management**: These patterns help traders manage risk more effectively by providing clear signals for placing stop-loss orders. For example, in a Morning Star pattern, a stop-loss can be placed below the low of the second candle to protect against false signals.
4. **Increased Confidence**: Understanding and utilising Morning Star and Evening Star patterns can boost a trader's confidence. These patterns have been tested and proven over time, providing reliable signals for market reversals.

Mastering the Morning Star and Evening Star patterns is crucial for traders to maximise leverage at market reversals. These robust three-day reversal signals identify changes in trends early, allowing traders to take opportunistic trades. Traders can use these patterns to complement their market analysis when trading, which naturally leads to better execution and improved risk management. However, whether you are a beginner or an expert trader or simply learning how to trade online understanding, following the patterns of Morning Star and Evening Star can boost your trading success rate and profitability.

Candlestick Reversal Signals: Overview and Importance for Traders

Candlestick patterns are essential tools for traders, providing visual insights into market sentiment and potential trend reversals. Here, we'll summarise key reversal signals—Dark Cloud Cover, Piercing Line, and Harami patterns—highlighting their criteria, significance, and why traders should pay attention to them.

Dark Cloud Cover

This is one of the most common bearish reversal patterns that traders anticipate during a bullish trend. This began with a long white candle representing strong bullish strength. This gives an initial indication that the bullish sentiment from the previous day will persist when the market opens higher than the previous day's high. Yet, this effort is quickly negated as the stock closes within the lower half of the white candlestick body. This change in momentum shows that the bulls are weakening and the bears are taking over.

When the Dark Cloud Cover appears, traders should take this as an important signal indicating the potential end of an uptrend and the onset of a bearish phase. This pattern recognition can alert traders to close their long positions to avoid losses, or even initiate short positions. If the pattern appears with high trading volume and is joined by other indicators (like a stochastic reading indicating overbought levels) then this can certainly boost its reliability.

Piercing Line

The Piercing Line pattern is the bullish counterpart of the Dark Cloud Cover occurring at the bottom of a downtrend. This pattern starts with a black candle that signals strong bearish emotions. The market opens the following day and opens lower, indicating that the selling will continue. The powerful buying interest, however, pushes the price higher by the day's close and leaves a candle that closes well embedded into the body of the previous day's dark candle.

This pattern is a critical indicator for traders, suggesting a potential bullish reversal. If a Piercing Line pattern occurs, it signals that the bulls have started to take control. This signal can be used by traders to initiate long positions, expecting the prices to increase. Like the Dark Cloud Cover, the increased trading volume and oversold stochastics substantially increase the reliability of the Piercing Line pattern.

Harami Pattern (Bullish and Bearish)

The Harami pattern is another potent reversal signal, characterised by a large candle followed by a smaller candle that is entirely within the body of the previous candle. The term 'Harami' means 'pregnant' in Japanese, describing the pattern's appearance as if a smaller candle is contained within the larger one.

Bullish Harami

A downtrend includes a dark long candle that imitates bearish sentiment. The next candle that forms is a Harami, which is a white (or another dark) candle, within the body of the previous day's black (closing down) candle, suggesting indecision and lack of selling pressure. The chart indicates that a reversal may take place and the downtrend could be over.

Traders should consider the Bullish Harami as a signal for a possible long entry or to exit short positions. It is an even stronger pattern when the white candle closes solidly above the upper range of the bearish candle and is accompanied by heavier trade volume on the second day.

Bearish Harami

The Bearish Harami, on the other hand, will appear during an uptrend with a long white candle which gives a clear sign of market bias towards buyers. A smaller dark candle appears in the body of the preceding white candlestick symbolising that buying pressure is waning. This pattern represents a potential bullish reversal.

Given how widespread it is, and certainly because of its implications for a trend reversal, traders can benefit greatly from knowing what a Bearish Harami looks like. This could be a signal for traders to take profit on long positions or potentially adopt short positions. The pattern has even more credibility if the close of the dark candle lies close to the lower range of the white candle's body and there is a large volume spike on the second day.

Importance for Traders

The most important thing for traders is to understand and identify these candlestick patterns. The patterns provide visual clues about market sentiment and potential reversals which a trader can view to guide trades and their entries and exits into positions. The above signalling system can help traders predict market movements, better manage risk, and maximise profits by incorporating these signals into their trading strategies.

The Morning and Evening Star candlestick patterns are real three-day reversal formations that both demonstrate the power of working with the candlesticks. A bullish reversal pattern, called the Morning Star, occurs following a downtrend and includes a large dark candle, a small-bodied candle with short shadows, and a large white candle. This pattern suggests a change in sentiment from bearish to bullish. On the other hand, an Evening

Star indicates a bearish reversal. The first candle is a long white candle, with a small-bodied second candle followed by a black long candle for the third one signalling a shift of sentiment from bullish to bearish.

To sum up, candlestick patterns such as the Dark Cloud Cover, Piercing Line and Harami are powerful tools for traders, able to give insights into market psychology and potential trend changes. Through the mastery of these patterns, traders can improve their trading performance and risk management and increase their chances of success in financial markets.

❑

8

Support and Resistance

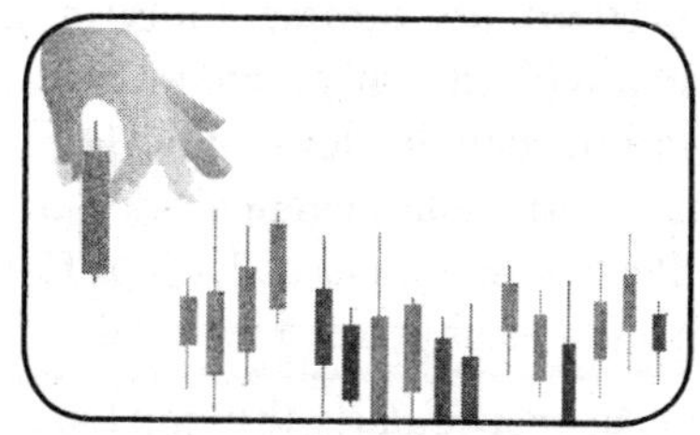

Prices move fast in a dynamic equities market. These changes occur in response to company announcements, broader investor sentiments, and media reports. While the fundamentals evaluate a company's potential over the long term, they do not translate into short-term price action. But it is instead how traders and investors respond to these fundamentals on a long-term basis that ultimately affects stock price.

The market would work quite differently if stock prices were determined only by fundamentals. The stock prices reflect all available information in real time. Prices would adjust quickly to new information, leading to continuous price updates rather than stable equilibrium. As shown in the prices table above, stock prices are subjected to constant evaluation as investors re-evaluate a business.

This is why charts and technical analysis are important. Technical analysis is the study of past market data, primarily in terms of price and volume, to predict future price movements. It works because price patterns in recent history can be used to predict future price movements.

Candlestick charts are favoured by traders as they provide a visual representation of the price ranges over a specific time period, such as a day, week or month. The body of the candlestick represents the open and closing prices for that trading session, while the wicks show the high and low prices.

Candlestick patterns are simple tools to illustrate market sentiment and the possibility of reversing trends. For instance, a series of long white candlesticks indicates a strong uptrend whereas a sequence of long dark candlesticks shows a downtrend. Also, certain candlestick patterns like Doji or Hammer can signal market indecision and possible trend reversal.

Technical analysis, particularly through the use of candlestick charts allows traders to generate trading signals based on market sentiment and price patterns. Technical analysis provides traders with decision-making tools to identify entry and exit points. It is applicable across various financial markets, including stocks, currencies and commodities.

The illustration below shows the movement of a stock price in a sideways range that fluctuates back and forth over two sets of prices. The upper boundary of the range represents a price level where supply meets or exceeds demand, and is called a 'resistance level'. At this stage, the stock falls due to bearish pressure. Conversely, when the stock falls towards the lower boundary, the sentiment changes radically and demand surpasses supply, forming a support level.

First, we will learn how to draw the support and resistance levels.

One of the most important tasks in technical analysis includes plotting support and resistance levels on a chart, which are key standpoints while determining price reversal points. To plot these levels, the traders need to first detect swing highs and lows on the chart. Swing highs = resistance; swing lows = support. Traders link these highs and lows to visualise the trajectory of price movements. Also, traders draw horizontal lines across price levels where the price has struggled to move beyond (resistance) or has bounced back from (support). These levels are considered strong because they have been validated multiple times. Additionally, candlestick patterns such as Doji or small-bodied candles can confirm support and resistance levels. In essence, plotting support and resistance levels is essential for traders aiming to anticipate price movements.

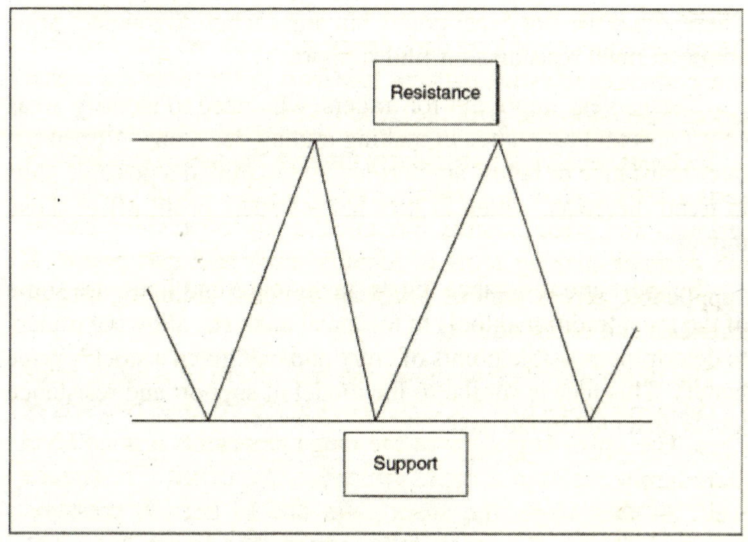

Support and Resistance

Support and resistance levels are an essential part of technical analysis, reflecting areas on a price chart where buying interest (support) or selling interest (resistance) is strong. These levels are often used by traders to find spots for entries or exits in the process of price action. These levels are not static and can evolve over time with market changes.

This is basically about human nature and the tendency of the price to oscillate between levels of support and resistance. Traders are likely to remember past price levels when a significant trading activity occurred. Traders who missed an earlier opportunity to buy a stock at a lower price may eagerly jump in when the price retraces to that level again. The collective actions of traders will lead to the price swinging back and forth between the support and resistance levels.

Support and resistance are identified using various tools such as trendlines, moving averages, and Fibonacci retracement levels. These zones are not exact points but areas where we expect price action to meet resistance or find support.

This is very important for traders, who need to identify areas of support and resistance in making trading decisions. A breakout over resistance or below support levels can hint at a possible shift in trend direction, which in turn helps traders profit off of those moves.

Support and resistance levels, including trend lines, are some of the most traditional tools in technical analysis, allowing traders to determine possible points of entry and exit given a stock's price history. This idea is similar to the model of support and resistance levels provided in the past.

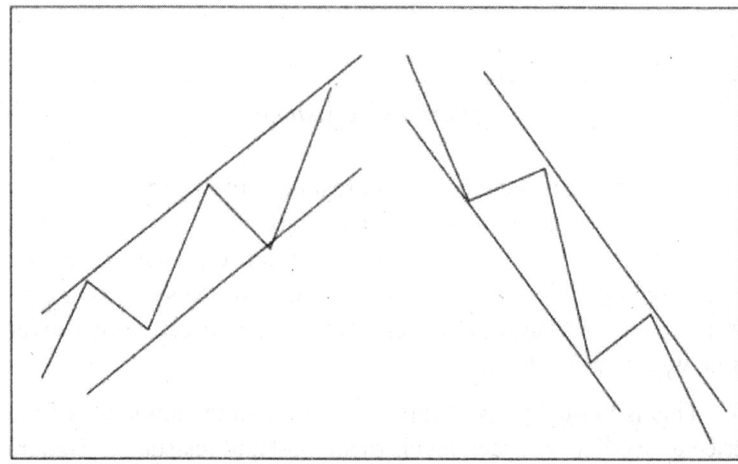

Trend channels

If the trend is up, then the support line goes under the price lows showing us a point where we expect to find buying interest. In a downtrend, the resistance line will be placed above the price highs indicating a level where selling pressure could kick in. The price flows between these lines to form a financial canal, aligning with the general direction of the trend.

Traders need to realise that they are not trading the stock itself, but they are trading the emotions and sentiments of people in the market. Understanding this can enable traders to accurately read market signals and make more informed trading decisions.

Several key points about trendlines are worth noting:

- Trendlines can be horizontal or sloping, depending on the angle of the price movement.
- The strength of a trendline is often determined by the number of times the price touches or tests the line. The more the touches, the stronger the support or resistance.
- When a support trendline is breached, it may act as a resistance trendline going forward, and vice versa. This reversal in role indicates a potential shift in market sentiment.

Understanding and utilising trendlines can enhance a trader's ability to navigate the market and identify profitable trading opportunities. By incorporating trendlines into their analysis, traders can gain valuable insights into market dynamics and improve their overall trading strategy.

When considering resistance and support levels, candlestick patterns can provide crucial insights for traders. Here's a deeper dive into how these patterns can be interpreted in relation to these key levels:

1. **Confirmation of Support or Resistance:** Further, the strength or weakness of support and resistance levels can be

confirmed by candlestick patterns. When a Doji or a small-bodied candle forms at a support level, it indicates indecision in the market and that the support level might hold firm. Conversely, a bearish candle might show that the resistance has been breached, and if we observe a strong bullish candle, it could signal a complete breakthrough of the resistance level.

2. **Reversal Signals:** Certain candlestick patterns serve as reversal signals at support or resistance levels. For instance, a bullish reversal pattern like a Bullish Engulfing Pattern at a support level could indicate a potential price reversal to the upside. Conversely, a bearish reversal pattern like a Bearish Engulfing Pattern at a resistance level might suggest a possible reversal to the downside.

3. **Strength of Support or Resistance:** Candlestick type and size can also signal the strength of support or resistance levels. A candle with a long tail that touches a strategic support level provides evidence that there is indeed a strong buying interest in this level, confirming it as an important support level. Conversely, a long upper shadow on candles shows that the price tested resistance but failed to break through, suggesting a strong resistance level.

4. **Volume Confirmation:** Volume can further confirm the validity of support or resistance levels when combined with candlestick patterns. For instance, a breakout above a resistance level with high volume could indicate strong buying interest, supporting the likelihood of a continued uptrend.

Candlestick patterns can provide valuable insights into the behaviour of traders at support and resistance levels. By interpreting these patterns in the context of these key levels, traders can make more informed decisions about entry and exit points, as well as the overall direction of the market.

Moving Average

Moving averages (MAs) are frequently used in technical analysis as a way to smooth out price data, albeit by calculating average prices over a specified period. They are called 'moving' because they keep changing (via continuous recalculations) as new data comes in, and hence give a refreshed view of the direction of the market. There are many moving average types but the two common ones are simple moving average (SMA) and exponential moving averages (EMA).

The SMA is simply the sum of a security's closing prices divided by the number of periods, e.g. 10, 50, 200, etc. This average is plotted on the chart and moves with the price, which can help illustrate the prevailing trend. While SMAs effectively smooth out price data, they do not respond quickly to sudden price movements because each data point carries equal weight.

Conversely, because the EMA assigns greater weight to recent prices, it reacts quicker to changes in price direction. EMA is calculated by assigning more value to the most recent data points when calculating the average, which makes it react faster to price changes than SMA. Some traders prefer EMAs for short-term analysis while preferring SMAs for long-term analysis, though in both situations the other can still be beneficial based on their trading strategy.

Moving averages provide a more accurate reading of how a stock or market is trending by smoothing out price fluctuations, making it easier to identify short-term direction. They are widely used in technical trading, often generating real-time alerts when moving average crossovers occur. For instance, buying when a short-term moving average crosses above a longer-term average, and selling/going short when the opposite is true. In shorter timeframes, this approach can be delayed. Using a longer time frame can mitigate this issue because it plays to the strengths of the RSI in conjunction with a longer-term moving average trend filter.

But in the context of candlestick signals, moving averages can enhance investment results. Moving averages play a crucial role in identifying trends and establishing support and resistance levels. The simple moving average (SMA) along with the exponential moving average (EMA), are used for this particular strategy. For more in-depth reading on the subject of EMA, please refer to other technical analysis resources.

Moving averages are used in various ways by traders. One common strategy is to look for crossovers between shorter-term and longer-term moving averages. For example, when the shorter-term EMA crosses above the longer-term SMA, it may signal a bullish trend reversal, known as a 'golden cross'. Conversely, when the shorter-term EMA crosses below the longer-term SMA, it may indicate a bearish trend reversal, known as a 'death cross'.

Moving averages as a support or resistance area: The price often rebounds against the moving average in an uptrend (the moving average acts as support). The moving average can work as a barrier that resists the breakout where the price tries to go higher in a downtrend. These levels can be used by traders to enter or exit trades, relying on the moving average to serve as a reference when making trading decisions.

Overall, the moving average is a flexible segment of technical analysis that offers traders signals and trends in the market, as well as potential entries and exits. Through an understanding of how moving averages are created and used, traders can use the information to their advantage enabling them to make better informed trades.

Candlestick patterns are renowned for revealing emerging trends and exposing directional market dynamics. Candlesticks signal great potential trend shifts rather than specific entry points for trades. Whenever price targets are set, traders often rely on other technical analysis tools, with larger moving averages being one of the most common methods. Since stock prices typically reflect the operational performance of associated companies, traders may use fundamental analysis as an alternative to identifying technical crossovers.

❑

9

The Trading Psychology

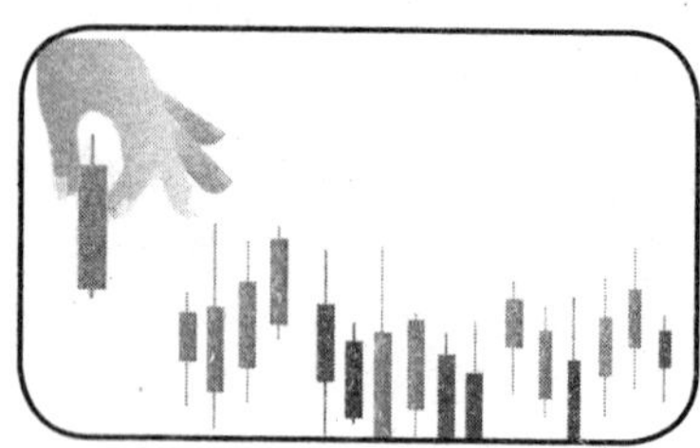

To trade effectively, it is essential to integrate candlestick signals with other technical analysis tools. We have explored the major candlestick patterns and how they can be used in conjunction with traditional Western technical analysis. The accuracy of these signals in predicting market reversals is quite high, especially when multiple signals align to confirm a reversal. For example, the Morning Star and Evening Star patterns become significantly more reliable when the middle day features a one-day candlestick reversal signal, such as a Hammer or Hanging Man. Similarly, a Bullish Engulfing pattern forming precisely at a known support level enhances the credibility of the impending reversal.

You have insider knowledge, which gives you a competitive advantage over your competition. You will also be able to avoid one of the central mistakes when trading—attempting to 'catch a falling knife' rather than waiting for a more reliable signal just because it has lost 10%. A stock that has lost 10% can just as easily fall another 20%, or it could rebound and enter a new upward move. The catch is that you cannot foresee which of the two results will actually come to light unless more analysis is done. Instead, observe the candle patterns and trust the signals they provide. In order to enter the market, we need similar signals: clear buy signals that should be confirmed by indicators like stochastics and a trading pattern. Using these principles in line with the tools available to you will allow you to make better and more strategic trading decisions.

Getting Real—Candlesticks Fail, Too!: It would be ideal if candlestick signals were 100% effective, if they never failed, and acted as the ultimate magic tool for trading. Unfortunately, that is not the case. While candlestick signals are highly effective and have stood the test of time for over four centuries, they are not infallible. If they were not effective, they would not have persisted for so long. They provide a high probability of indicating reversal points, but the key word here is 'probability'.

There will be times when everything aligns perfectly: you have the ideal candlestick signal, stochastics are in the right place, the signal is confirmed, and you enter the trade—only to see the stock move in the opposite direction. This is an unavoidable part of trading.

Trading, much like running a business, involves periods of loss. Any successful business person understands that occasional losses are normal and expected. The goal is to ensure that your gains outweigh these periodic setbacks. This philosophy is crucial for traders as well. Losses are an inherent part of trading, and they cannot be avoided.

You cannot control the market environment. Even if a stock presents an excellent buy scenario, external factors, such as a broader market downturn, can exert pressure and negate the positive setup with negative signals. In such situations, the market has proved your initial analysis wrong, and as a trader, you face a crucial decision point.

Ride Your Ego: Ego can lead traders to disregard clear signals and hold onto losing positions despite the market moving against your position. You believe that you understand the market better than anyone else does. And this feeling makes you keep holding the shares, hoping that one sweet day it will turn around and get back to the winning side. But this method is not without its dangers. The market operates independently of personal beliefs and sticking with losing trades can compound losses over time. The more you remain entrenched in this position, the deeper your losses eat into your capital and undermine your confidence.

Acknowledge the Failure: Recognising that this trade failed and swiftly admitting that this trade went wrong is not a sign of weakness, but quite simply prudent trading. When you identify that the market is moving against your position, you can quickly reduce your losses. Exit the trade with a minimal loss quickly to preserve your capital and live to fight another good battle. In this way, you will always be in the position to take advantage of any subsequent favourable signal without risking either your capital or emotional energy. This principle lies at the heart of successful trading—cutting losses short while allowing profits to run. It is this practice that distinguishes profitable traders from those who dig themselves deeper into losses.

Many traders fall into the trap of equating a failed trade with personal failure. They find it difficult to accept that, despite their technical knowledge, they can still encounter losing trades. Overcoming this pitfall is essential for trading success. It is not easy, but it is necessary. Without the ability to accept small losses, no amount of candlestick or technical analysis knowledge will make your portfolio grow.

The old saying 'Cut your losses short and let your profits run' is a golden rule of trading. So, the question is where to set your stop losses: at 2%, 5% or 10%? Many technical analysis books list a verifiable percentage, but to the candlestick trader, these figures serve nothing. Truly the success of a trader depends on this. When and where to apply stop-loss is however not an easy question. Instead, one must ask some fundamental questions and find appropriate solutions. This basic knowledge or information is what you need to tip the scales in your favour when trading, ensuring you can effectively manage trades and achieve long-term profits.

In candlestick trading, going long in the stock is indicated when a buy signal appears, suggesting that stocks will move up. To defend against losses, the trader puts a stop-loss at a level where the candlestick buy signal would be invalidated. In contrast, the candlestick trader shorts the stock when a sell signal is generated by using a bearish reversal pattern—indicating an upcoming downtrend. The stop-loss is set at a point where it would invalidate the candlestick sell signal, ensuring that the trader captures potential profits even if the market moves against the trade.

❑

10

Reward-to-Risk Ratio

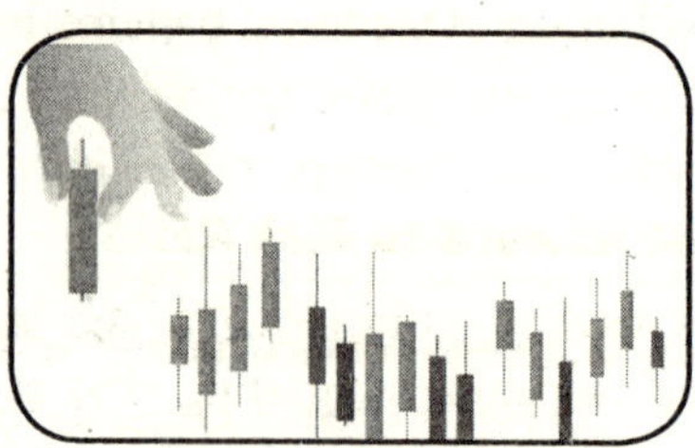

Now let us delve into some tips for you to enhance your investment journey and make more calculated profits. A fundamental aspect to consider in this journey of making profits is to look at the reward-to-risk ratio.

Reward-to-Risk Ratio

The reward-to-risk ratio is a basic concept of trading and investing. It indicates the profit that can be obtained on any trade against the loss. It has a vital role in assisting traders to be able to determine whether a trade is worth the risk by assessing that situation.

What is the Reward-to-Risk Ratio and How to Calculate it?

A reward-to-risk ratio is determined by the three important price points of any trade.

Entry Point: The price at which you enter the trade, based on a particular trading signal or strategy. For example, a confirmed candlestick pattern signalling an impending price move.

Stop-Loss Point: This is the price level where you will close out your trade to minimise losses if the market moves against your expectations. The stop-loss acts as a safety mechanism to save your capital and minimise losses.

Target Price: The point at which you plan to exit the trade according to your trading rules. Typically, this is set at a prior high, resistance level or other technical patterns indicative of the price direction.

Advantages of the Reward-to-Risk Ratio

Informed Decision-Making: Before taking a trade, utilising the reward-to-risk ratio helps in better decision-making. It helps assess whether the potential payoff is worth the risk behind it. If the risk of loss for you is @10 and the reward potential is only @5, that makes your reward-to-risk ratio 0.5:1 which is unfavourable. Traders like to see at least 2:1 ratios, where the potential reward is two points for every point lost.

Capital Preservation: The most significant of them all is to use the reward-to-risk ratio for capital protection. By setting a stop-loss point, you define the maximum amount that you're willing to lose on every trade. This is a disciplined way to avoid holding onto losing trades with the hope that they will turn around resulting in the possibility of heavy losses.

Consistency and Discipline: The reward-to-risk ratio makes you a consistent, disciplined trader. It allows traders to adhere to their trading plan and mitigate emotional decision-making. Trading these ratios means traders are far more likely to gain consistent success over the long term and not be wholly reliant on sporadic big wins.

Enhanced Profitability: A high reward-to-risk ratio increases the likelihood of long-term profitability in trading. Even with a lower win rate, trades with a good ratio yield higher profits than losses. For example, a 3:1 reward-to-risk ratio would allow you to be profitable even if you're right less than half the time.

Risk Management: The reward-to-risk ratio is a critical risk management element. Then you can check if a trade complies with your individual and comprehensive risks score. Tracking the ratio allows you to maintain better control of your portfolio and not expose yourself too much.

Practical Example

Let us consider a potential trade with the following price points:

- **Entry Point: ₹100**
- **Stop-Loss Point: ₹95 (limiting your loss to ₹5)**
- **Target Point: ₹110 (potential gain of ₹10)**

The trade in this instance offers a 2:1 potential reward-risk ratio. This indicates that the potential profit is twice the amount of the potential loss, which is considered favourable.

To sum up, the reward-to-risk ratio is a useful tool for traders. It not only aids in making informed trading decisions but is also crucial for risk management and capital preservation. Traders are advised to pursue trades where ratios are in their favour, as this increases profitability and chances of lasting success in buying or selling commodities.

Do Not Turn Your Trade Into Investments

One of the biggest mistakes traders make is turning a trade into an investment. In normal conditions, they could potentially take advantage of an oversold condition or market panic by buying the dip, with the entry, target and stop-loss points in mind. Confident in the stock's potential rally, the trader hesitates when the stock starts to decline and crosses its stop-loss point. Despite knowing that selling and cutting losses is a wise decision, hope clouds their mind telling them to hold onto their position. As the stock continues to fall, they rationalise their decision by convincing themselves of the company's fundamental strength, sometimes even buying more in order to average up.

This approach can lead to several problems from a trader's perspective: loss of control over a significant portion of their portfolio (money is locked in that depreciating investment), missed opportunities elsewhere, and significant declines in invested capital. The key lesson is to avoid turning a losing trade into a long-term investment. If candlestick signals invalidate the trade, it is important to close the position and wait for another buying opportunity.

Let's get through an example with the story of Raj, a trader who had to learn the hard way about the difference between a trade and an investment.

Raj had been studying the market for several months and he believed that his trading strategy was good enough to succeed. He saw that one of the stocks, TechVision (which is a popular tech company) had fallen drastically one day due to panic selling, as indicated by oversold conditions in the stochastics. Raj saw this as a perfect opportunity. He detected a robust candlestick buy signal and decided to enter the trade.

Raj entered the trade at $100 a share with a goal of $120 and a stop-loss set at $95. To his delight, the stock initially rose as anticipated and he was validated in his analysis. Raj felt good about his decision as TechVision's price reached $110. However, market conditions quickly changed and TechVision's stock price began to decline sharply as liquidity concerns surfaced.

Despite having a stop-loss point at 95$, Raj hesitated as the stock price approached that point. Somewhere deep inside, an intuitive feeling urged him to wait a little longer. As the stock fell to $94, Raj still did not sell—after all, TechVision was a good company with great fundamentals according to him. He held the stock, hoping for a turnaround.

As the days turned into weeks, the stock fell even further to $80. Raj was losing money in his portfolio and felt cornered. He had put his capital in a losing trade, had missed other trading opportunities, and with the passage of time, his confidence diminished. Even though the losses were racking up, Raj doubled down and purchased additional shares at $80 in anticipation that averaging down would lower his overall cost.

However, TechVision stock plummeted further to $70. Raj lost money because he decided to turn a trade into an investment. Regrettably, he did not stick to the original plan and close positions at his stop-loss point. This was a painful lesson earned through experience. And he paid the price of retaining an incorrect position.

The most important realisation Raj came to was that trading is all about discipline. You need to be able to accept a small loss when the trade goes against you and move on. Letting a losing trade become your pet investment can be economically and psychologically taxing. Raj vowed that he would never allow hope to cloud his judgement in trading, and came to appreciate why discipline is so important (in fact critical) for long-term success as a trader.

Avoid Trading Low-volume Stocks

Low-volume stocks present a multitude of challenges that can significantly impact your trading journey over time.

For one, low-volume stocks often have poor liquidity. Liquidity refers to how easily one can buy or sell a stock without impacting the price of that stock! When a stock has high liquidity, you can purchase any amount with minimal delay. On the other hand, low-volume stocks usually have fewer participants resulting in wider bid-ask spreads. This means that you may have to sell for a lower price or buy at a higher rate than what your expectations were, reducing the potential profits.

Secondly, low-volume stocks are prone to price manipulations compared to the highly-traded market which experiences frequent price swings due to rapid buying and selling. When fewer shares are being traded, it takes less capital to make the stock price move sharply. This can lure manipulative traders in, who artificially inflate and deflate the process to distort the true market direction. Thus, traders may find themselves caught in price spikes or crashes that do not reflect the true value of the stock, leading to unexpected losses.

Furthermore, it can be difficult to analyse low-volume stocks with technical indicators. Basically, most of the technical analyses utilise historic price and volume data to generate signals. However, low-volume stocks have sparse trading activity resulting in limited data. This scarcity of data increases the likelihood of false signals, making it difficult to predict future price moves. This, therefore, increases the risk of making suboptimal trading decisions.

Take for instance the journey of a trader named Priya, with a few examples to illustrate these points. One day, Priya made up her mind to trade BioGenix, a small biotech company that had recently experienced some positive news. BioGenix was thinly traded, logging a few thousand shares of volume each day. Motivated by the same news, Priya bought 1,000 shares each at $10.

But when she decided to sell her shares a few days later, she ran into many issues. The bid-ask spread was wide, with the best bid at $9.50 and the best ask at $10.50. This meant that she would have to sell her shares at a price far below what she had initially expected and make an immediate loss. Furthermore, the low volume meant that it took her longer to sell those shares.

Eventually, she ended up selling her shares at an average price of $9.40.

Priya had also noticed that BioGenix's stock price was incredibly volatile during this time frame, with news-independent mega-swings taking place frequently. She would later find out these moves were just a few large trades, highlighting the susceptibility of low-volume stocks to price manipulation. Priya realised that trading low-volume stocks exposed her to additional risks and eroded her profits.

To avoid falling into trading traps, traders should stick with more liquid stocks. Because of the higher liquidity, price movements are more reliable, and technical analysis signals will work better. This will help you to increase the likelihood of executing trades at your desired prices, protect yourself against price manipulation, and provide a better knowledge base for making informed trade decisions from stronger data.

To recap, stay away from low-volume stocks to limit risks and enhance the potential for trading success!

Don't Hesitate to Enter the Market

Though they recognise a good signal, many traders still hesitate to enter the market at the opportune moment due to a lack of confidence. A trader might have countless reasons for not taking action: they may rely too heavily on opinions from online chat groups, second-guess themselves with unnecessary paper trades, or be swayed by some influential voices in the media predicting market downturns. They may even ignore a clear sell signal because everybody else is buying, or cease trading due to personal superstitions or trivial reasons.

This is particularly applicable in candlestick trading, where extensive analysis goes into interpreting market formations. Because of this knowledge, traders can confidently identify setups that signal higher likelihoods of market reversals. If the signal fails to materialise, exit the trade with a minimal loss. As such, it is essential to trade confidently and overcome risk aversion. Taking decisive actions is crucial and winning in the market isn't merely about internal confidence but about strategies and decisions.

Always believe in price action trading. Here's what it is and why you should believe in it.

Price action trading (PAT) is a form of technical analysis that evokes both awe and confusion in equal measures among the uninitiated. Price action traders look to time an entry on the back of movements detected in candlestick formations, support and resistance levels, trendlines or chart patterns like head and shoulders or triangles.

Price action trading is based on the idea that all relevant information to a security's market price is reflected in its price movements. This focuses on monitoring and interpreting how prices act at significant levels and within different patterns. Through the observation of price action, traders aim to develop trading strategies and forecast future prices.

Several key elements define price action trading:

1. **Candlestick Patterns**: Traders analyse candlestick formations to identify potential reversal or continuation signals. Patterns like Doji, Hammer, engulfing patterns, and pin bars are among those commonly used.
2. **Support and Resistance**: Price action traders identify significant levels where the price has historically reacted, such as support (where buying interest may increase) and resistance (where selling pressure may increase).
3. **Trendlines and Channels:** Drawing trendlines helps traders visualise the direction and strength of a trend. Channels, which involve parallel trendlines, can indicate potential trading ranges or trends.

4. **Chart Patterns**: Patterns like triangles, head and shoulders, double tops or bottoms, and flags are observed to predict potential breakouts or reversals.

Price action trading offers several advantages:

Simplicity: By using only the single most important factor, the price itself, it simplifies trade to its pure form without complicated tools and complex models.

Transparency: When traders observe price movements and patterns directly, they have a clearer view of market sentiment and dynamics.

Versatility: Price action principles are universal tools that can be applied to any timeframe or asset class, allowing for a wide range of trading styles and market environments.

Less Lag: Typically, in technical indicators, there is a lag between the movement of prices and their interpretation on an indicator level; this makes price action more immediate.

Risk Management: Traders can set optimal stop-loss orders and manage risk more effectively, by concentrating on critical levels and patterns.

Overall, price action trading is beneficial for traders looking to develop a deeper understanding of market behaviour and make informed trading decisions based on observable price patterns and trends.

In the end, let's talk about trading plans and journals.

A trading plan and journal are essential tools for any trader, providing structure, discipline and a framework for success in the financial markets.

For any trader looking to succeed in the ever-changing and often unpredictable world of financial markets, a trading plan and journal are both essential tools. A trading plan is essentially a strategic blueprint outlining your approach to trading along with an outline of all the goals and tactics that will help drive home this approach. It includes key elements such as trading strategies (technical or fundamental for example), how to manage potential losses, AKA risk management protocols, and different methodologies for market analysis. A trading plan establishes structure and discipline, provides guidelines for setting goals and defines risk tolerance levels along with entry and exit requirements.

Having a trading plan offers several key benefits, foremost among them being inculcation of discipline. Follow a predefined set of rules and strategies to avoid making decisions out of fear or greed. Consistency in trading decisions is also a major advantage. A viable plan helps traders to trade consistently based on a particular methodology, and this is the key aspect of succeeding in the markets over time. In addition, a trading plan places a strong emphasis on risk management by determining how much capital to allocate per trade and where stop losses should be placed against adverse moves within the market.

The trading plan is then complimented by a trade journal which should be a comprehensive record of all trades. It includes specific details like the trade date, instrument traded, position sizes, entry and exit prices, as well as why the given trade was taken. In addition to these basic details, a trading journal also records emotional elements of the trade by recording the trader's mindset and whether emotions played a role in making decisions. Through this process, I aim to help traders understand the psychology of their actions and inactions so that they can improve their emotional discipline while trading.

The trading journal performs many functions, but among the more important ones is maintaining a trade log to analyse your performance. Traders can gain a lot from systematically recording every trade, wins or losses, and analysing the outcomes to develop an understanding of why trades worked out (or why they did not). By regularly reviewing their entries, traders can maintain a disciplined approach and strive for consistency. This not only enhances performance but also contributes to the development of a successful mindset in the competitive world of trading. It also fosters accountability as traders hold themselves responsible for trading actions.

As it is easy to note, a trading plan and journal are not only knowledge tools but are essential for any trader. They offer the blueprint needed to navigate the labyrinth of financial markets effectively. It helps them develop and refine their decision-making processes, improve consistency in their trading approach, and eventually work towards meeting some of the goals that they may have set for themselves as traders by defining strategies, managing risks, and documenting trades taken with outcomes.

❑

11

Conclusion

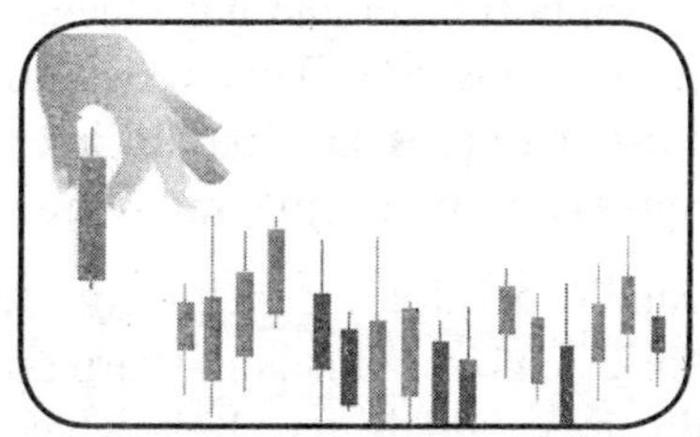

Candlestick trading is a strong analytical tool that has stood the test of time, seamlessly integrated with modern trading insights. It offers an excellent framework for navigating the complexities of financial markets. This involves reading price action through candlestick patterns and identifying support and resistance levels on charts. The advantages of candlestick trading go beyond just technical analysis. It provides a foundation to shape broader principles essential for successful trading practices.

A major benefit of using candlesticks is that they provide traders with visual representation and insights into market sentiment. For example, candlestick patterns such as Doji, Engulfing pattern and Hammer give insights into the market psychology at specific moments. A Doji candlestick indicates indecision and possible reversal while a Bullish Engulfing pattern suggests strong buying interest overcoming prior selling pressure. Traders who can recognise these patterns can anticipate changes in market direction and then determine the most likely course of action they should take.

Besides, candlestick trading fosters a disciplined risk management technique through predefined rules associated with every candlestick pattern and formation. These rules typically include criteria for entry, exit and stop-loss positioning. This method helps traders to minimise risk with the use of a fixed price point setting for the execution of trades. For instance, a trader might only wish to go long if a Bullish Engulfing pattern is confirmed at a key support level and has placed stop-loss orders just below the recent swing low. This systematic process leads to higher risk-adjusted returns and builds internal strength by preventing you from taking impulsive trades out of fear or greed.

In addition, candlestick trading helps you better understand how markets and prices move. This is in sharp contrast to trading using lagging indicators, which may hide what the markets are currently doing; candlestick analysis shows you supply and demand dynamics as they unfold. This allows traders to change their tactics in real time according to shifting market conditions, capitalising on developing chart formations and trends. This type of agility is important in turbulent markets because you can quickly make necessary adjustments to seize opportunities or preserve your investments effectively amidst market turbulence.

Candlestick trading offers significant advantages in terms of its versatility across various timeframes and financial instruments. Regardless of whether you are trading stocks, forex commodities or cryptocurrencies the same analytical principles still apply. Traders can customise their strategies to fit different market conditions, from short-term scalping tactics to long-term trend following. It allows traders to build diversified portfolios, and trade multiple asset classes, contributing to higher trading revenues.

Mastering candlestick patterns goes beyond technical skill—it also promotes a continuous process to improve trading skills. Traders who have been successful over prolonged periods will develop an acute sense of subtle patterns in price movements. They develop their skill for cracking the code of market signals, using historical price data and current events in markets to make trading decisions. This continuous learning and application of strategies allows traders to keep abreast of market developments, while strategically positioning themselves for success over the long term.

In addition, candlestick trading aligns closely with behavioural finance theory by acknowledging the effects of human psychology on price movements. Candlestick patterns portray the market emotions of fear, greed and delirium among other things. Through the analysis of such behaviour, traders have an opportunity to gain valuable information regarding sentiment within the marketplace which may be just as important if not more so than any fundamental or macroeconomic consideration. The holistic perception of market psychology enables traders to predict reversals, catch trend continuations, and profit from any market inefficiency.

In conclusion, candlestick trading offers multifaceted benefits that extend well beyond technical analysis. They serve as preventive measures in risk management, reading market psychology effectively, With the help of candlestick patterns, traders can have greater confidence and precision in navigating financial markets due to their visual clarity, leading to more actionable trading decisions. This technique allows you to focus on profit and risk-adjusted returns and inculcates the discipline and grit that is very much needed to succeed as a trader. The more that traders can adopt the subtleties of candlestick analysis and apply these principles to their trading strategies, the better-prepared they are to profit from market opportunities, aimed at sustainable long-term triumph in volatile financial markets.

❑